C000000792

URBAN ISIS

PART 2
REVOLUTIONARY

WILLIE GROSS JR.

Justice Now Books

Urban Isis
Part 2 Revolutionary
All Rights Reserved.
Copyright © 2021 Willie Gross Jr.
v2.0

Edited by Alanna Boutin © 2021

ISBN: 978-0-578-23961-3

Cover Photo © 2021 www.gettyimages.com. All rights reserved - used with permission.

Justice Now Books

PRINTED IN THE UNITED STATES OF AMERICA

Acknowledgments

For the perfect union of Mr. Willie Gross Sr. and Mrs. Loubertha Gross—I am forever indebted to you as parents. You were quality parents with gentle spirits. Daily, you've inspired me to be relevant to the simple task of being grateful. You made all around you better. Humility was your lesson, and the love of God and family was your curriculum. Both of you will be forever missed—may you both rest in peace.

For the countless number of first-class family and friends who've embraced me and became my shelter throughout the storms of life, I am grateful for your presence, advice, and companionship. You have exceeded all expectations. Your deeds were many, as were your sacrifices. I'm sure there exists no way to repay nor replace that which was so freely and genuinely given by you—except with my dedication to conveying what we all believe to be our truths about today's reality. Know this, I live to write your aches and pain—and share your burdens—for they are mine as well.

For the present and future purchasers of my Urban Isis Series—Thank You! My goal, future and present, is to subject you to the realism, then implore you to reflect upon the present-day task of pursuing a cause greater than oneself. I will never profess to have gotten the who's right, right because the goal of doing what's right is my only obligation. Yet, I hope that you'll join me in support of any or all of my future endeavors designed to assist others in need. You can visit www.urbanisis art gallery for updates and future projects. There are ways to support a cause by purchasing books and artwork from the website. Again, I thank you.

For the purpose that guided me toward writing, this burning desire is fueled by the muffled voices of a forgotten people, past and present. I am humbled by their audacity to hope that their cries and genius would no longer be as whispers in the wind. Today, their audacity to be geniuses are acknowledged, as are their tears. I am better because of your stories. Yet, I'm tirelessly motivated by the fact that a disenfranchised people are seated on a vicious path of renewed pledges by secret societies blowing silent whistles to their proxies.

Lastly, in defiance, I urge you to remain vigilant and to hold on to what God has prescribed for you — for there is none better to guide us. Every day, I awaken to see another sunrise on its way to another sunset. Then and there, I realize that we are all exactly where we are supposed to be in life. Be it your circumstances, good or bad, rich or poor . . . nothing is more important than our realization that God is the most merciful and brings rain down upon the just as well as the unjust. For this, I thank God for seating me in the right places, so I'd learn the importance of patience, perseverance, and prayer. Although my road traveled in this life may have been a rocky one, I now know those times were my tests.

Introduction

Let us, reader and writer, agree on only what's real, numbers, and reality, primarily because they don't lie! Tragically, the drug usage among our teenagers of today has steadily increased year after year after year. The problem with this reality is it infringes upon the productivity of our expected torchbearers of tomorrow — the dreamers, the inventors, the pioneers of new technologies that'll spearhead breakthroughs in scientific research, futuristically enabling this nation to remain ahead of and relevant to every other nation.

Yet, as a nation, it seems as though we won't decide which of the two is more important: the drugs or the torchbearers. It is one thing to say we are who we say we are as a nation; yet, we steadily and with regularity, do the opposite. So, we ask ourselves, those confused and concerned by these truths . . . *What's the plan?* Or, *who's doing the planning?*

Yes, politics, greed, economics, fear, arrogance, and hate . . . All recipes for the gradual destruction of a nation and its torchbearers! These are critical components designed to suppress the brilliance, idealism, and productivity of our young, bright minds. The critical thinkers in possession of solutions to common problems plaguing our society, our neighborhoods, our schools, and ultimately . . . our generations!

But, today, we're thinking critically! We'll start designing what our minds, hearts, and souls are in total agreement with. It's the right thing to do. We won't fool ourselves into selfish decisionmaking centered around who's right. We're thinking long-range, making decisions for the whole, predicated on solid advice in doing what's right!

Yes, it's fiction—only because we're living in a society controlled by a few—and their only concern is always *their* needs. So, to do what's right in this society would be to them, fictitious. Now, we've established that their fiction is really a reality in the real world, so let's talk building! No hidden agendas . . . hands on the table . . . real-life, drama-type of building.

Let's dream again; let's rewind our memories; let's go back to when all of us knew as preschoolers and young grade-schoolers what we wanted to be in life. Let's heal instead of kill the dreams of tomorrow. Feel me? Let's build this dynasty alongside James Johnson. Let's come together in our minds, then think critically about our tomorrows . . . our hopes, our struggles, our accomplishments, our defeats, our victories, and, yes, even our demise. But more importantly, let's leave something good behind. Let's do *that*!

Let's resolve to understand why we struggle, get it all out of our system, then never look back, because the struggle isn't our identity. It was only made to look that way. That's why we accepted it!

In essence, we tear down the fake, then replace it with the real. Let's not automatically think defeat when we go up against the powers that be! Remember, *they're* the reason why we're in this mess! Look, we're building in this book, the right way too, reality!

Let's realize our propensity to be a great people first; *then* we can talk that great nation stuff. Keep turning pages; you'll see, we're people building. This way, we can't lose because we must be a great people before we can be a great nation. You agree? But it's not going to be pretty. Old habits die hard! But they *do* die, and that's James Johnson's only concern!

Now, let all of us envision ourselves in powerful positions, just like the powerful people of today, then ponder . . . If *I* ruled the world, what would *I* do? Who would *I* be? What, then, would be *my* contribution to society? Imagine *that*!

Let's face reality . . . No matter how much good we do in life, it'll never be enough to satisfy the haters. It's what they do best. So keep turning pages to see how James dealt with those haters. How he masterfully played a game they invented.

Let's look at the big picture—the future! Let's all agree . . . Tomorrow is for those who prepare for it today. Let's begin with the real . . . "Urban Isis, Part 1: The Revolution"!

Chapter 1

The anticipation of the kill had silenced his foul mood. But time was short, so he had to make his move. Quick. As he cautiously navigated the Audi A8 through traffic, his eyes mechanically darted from mirror to mirror, crafting a getaway route. His adrenaline was turned all the way up, made evident by the beads of perspiration continuously trickling down his armpits. The highway he traveled on for the last ten minutes had finally deposited him at his destination.

Salvator drove into the driveway that Kane had been utilizing for the past two years. No vehicles were in the driveway, and nobody seemed to be home. Salvator was trying to pinpoint when they would be coming back. He waited an extra three hours until night had fallen, but no traffic was present at the home. Kane was nowhere in sight. Instinct made him exit the vehicle with deliberate haste. He was standing at the door in only a few strides.

Salvator opened the screen door, looked around for witnesses, and when he noticed none present, he kicked the door off its hinges. He moved through the home like the trained warrior he was, searching every room, corner, and closet. He took in the scattered clothing that appeared to have been tossed about as if someone had left in a hurry. As he continued to search, he picked up a picture of Kane and Diamond off the dresser, then slid it into his inside jacket pocket. Satisfied with what he knew to be the truth, he exited the home at a quickened pace.

Once he entered his vehicle, he backed out of the driveway, then headed for the interstate. He screwed the silencer off the 9-millimeter Sig and popped the clip out, laying the pistol, clip, and silencer in the console, then closing it. His thoughts were busy, so he turned the music down. Did Kane know he was coming? Again, Salvator opened the console; the pistol, clip, and silencer were now gone. He dialed James. The phone rang three times.

"Hello?"

"Everybody at the residence packed in a hurry," Salvator said, adjusting the clock to the right time.

"Sounds like somebody is guilty of something," James suggested.

"Any other avenues to explore?" He turned off the air conditioner.

"Let me do some searching. Maybe I can come up with something on where he might be headed," James stated.

"Give me a call when you need me." Salvator hung up the phone, then took the picture out of his jacket pocket. He stared at it for a long time, searing Diamond and Kane into his memory.

Ring, ring, ring . . .
"Hello?"
"Troy, what are you up to?" James inquired.

"Nothing much. Getting dressed to go to Club Ballers in search of my queen," Troy said.

"Got a few questions for you."

"Okay, shoot. You got my undivided attention."

"What's up with this dude Kane?" James asked.

"What do you want to know?" Troy curiously asked.

"You can begin with what his role is in the organization."

"He oversees four houses out in the East, and he's consistent with making us lots of money."

"How loyal is he?" James inquired.

Troy paused a few seconds. James had never asked a question for nothing. Something was up.

"To what degree?" Troy asked.

"To any degree, Troy. I never knew there were degrees of loyalty."

"This is not happening." Troy sighed. "He's been averaging between ten and eleven million dollars a month in Eastern New Orleans. And, considering the amount of product I'm giving him, he's always over my estimates."

"That doesn't answer the question of his loyalty, Troy. Could it be that you don't know the answer to the question?"

"It's hard to say because I can't compare him to Luqman, or me to you in that category."

"The question was one concerning his loyalty to *you*," James said. "Did you not bring him into our operation?"

"Yes. But I think more so because of his skills in the streets, and the fact that he was hungry like us," Troy replied.

"So, loyalty didn't factor into the decision to bring him on board?"

"Looking at it from that perspective, it was only a small amount considered, and that came from what I knew of him in the penitentiary."

"So, you would allow a snake into your home as a friend, because it allowed you to pick it up?"

Silence.

"Troy, you can never put a price tag on loyalty. Money will get you killed; loyalty will keep you safe. Kane possessed a key element, a key element that you mentioned, which would cause him to deceive us in the blink of an eye. You care to guess what that element is?" James asked.

"James, you taught me a long time ago about guessing. So, no."

"But what exactly did you learn?" James shot back.

"That a man who relies on a guess acts without the benefit of his intellect," Troy replied.

"So, what if your decision to allow Kane into our organization proved to be a costly one?"

"It would mean that I didn't give my intellect a chance to make the best decision, and that made me a guesser."

"You're right! You said he was hungry like us, yet we were never hungry. That element should never be present in an organization. There's simply no place for it. This is an organization, Troy, and it's about everybody doing what they're supposed to do, including you. Unorganized fools talk about being hungry. That only means that they will betray anyone at any time for any price."

"So, where is all this going?" Troy inquired.

"When is your next drop-off or pickup from Kane?" James asked.

"I dropped and picked up last week. Why?"

"Where did all this take place?"

"At his house on America Street in the East."

"How much did you drop off?"

"A hundred kilos."

"Well, Salvator just left that house, and Kane has left town in a hurry because of some other shit he got into. So we've taken a major hit in the process. Did Kane ever follow protocol like he was supposed to?"

"Not really," Troy said reluctantly.

"Not really? What's *that* supposed to mean, Troy?" James angrily stated.

"James, I stressed the importance of a legitimate business to him the last time we met, and he agreed to handle it."

"Do you know what a condition of a contract means?"

"Yes, I understand, James. Look, I fucked up. Now, where do we go from here?"

"From here, it seems you need a smaller role in the organization. Maybe a position of authority is something foreign to you," James said.

"Maybe it was a case of bad judgment!" Troy shot back.

"Maybe, but what's the first rule of the game?"

"Never give or front anyone something that can hurt you."

"So, what part of that did you violate?"

Troy thought about the question. He knew that a hundred kilos were nothing compared to what they had, so he didn't see it hurting them in any way. But somehow, he felt as if he was missing a piece of the whole equation, and James was about to punish him with it, and for it.

"Those hundred kilos didn't hurt, James." Troy knew it was a lame answer when it rolled off his tongue, but he had to say something.

"I pegged you to give a better response than that, Troy. I thought I taught you better."

"Sorry to disappoint you."

"Maybe there is such a thing as too much of a good thing," James said.

Troy decided to remain silent, sensing this could go on until the morning, and he had other plans for this night, like Club Ballers.

"I take your silence as an indication that you want to know how your friend hurt us, right?"

"No sense in guessing when the answer is close around."

"Do you know what a force field is, Troy?"

"Something to do with protection."

"It's *everything* to do with protection. I spent many years building that force field and survived countless wars because of the protection it provided. The force field is our laws, Troy. We don't turn that fuckin' protection off for anything or anybody! It goes off, all of us are vulnerable to the enemies that are lurking out there waiting to replace us. Deon, Luqman, Salvator, and I are sitting ducks because you decided to turn off the protection by going against the grain! I made you and Luqman come up with a business plan for a reason. *That's* your protection! If Kane made excuses about why he didn't put together a plan to get out of this rat race, then he planned to fail. You can't change a made-up mind, Troy. You didn't do what was best for the team, so you failed the team," James said solemnly.

"You're one hundred percent right, James," Troy said, feeling down.

"I wish I wasn't, li'l brother. There's no enjoyment in me having this conversation with you. I want to depend on you, but you left my back door wide open. How can I feel safe?"

Troy had nothing he could've said to those last words. He had left James's back door open. It was ringing in his head. Luqman had just spoken to him about the same issue.

Akbar was on his way to meet his longtime friend from Pakistan. He requested that they meet outside of New Orleans in anticipation of some future trouble because as long as he possessed the disc, he would be a marked man.

Ahmed lived in Baton Rouge, about forty-five minutes away from New Orleans, and would be a perfect place to hide or start a new life. He needed someone he could trust exclusively, and Ahmed was as loyal as they come. He owned his store and had a small family of three, counting himself, his wife, and twelve-year-old son.

Akbar pulled into the parking lot of a Waffle House located in LaPlace, Louisiana. Ahmed was seated in his 745 BMW talking on his cell phone. Akbar walked up to his car, then started tapping on the window, startling Ahmed. A smile ran across his face when he saw Akbar. He hung up the phone, then stepped out of the vehicle.

"As-salaamu alaikum," Ahmed greeted him.

"Wa alaikum as-salam," Akbar returned the greeting. "How's the family?"

"They're well, Alhamdulillah. How's everything with your family in Pakistan?" Ahmed asked.

"Still living amongst the believers, all praise to Allah."

"So, what's your big secret that has you dragging me all the way out here, Akbar?"

"I need your help in a very delicate situation that can be very good for us in the end," Akbar stated.

Ahmed began looking around, wondering what the flip side of the coin was going to be. There always is. "What's it going to cost, an arm or a leg?" he inquired.

"Well, you know it has its pros and cons, but nothing we're not used to," Akbar replied. "But first, here's a list of gadgets I need for you to get. I have to do a couple of days' worth of some more strategic things; then I'm coming to lie low in Baton Rouge a while. In the meantime, I need you to hold this little disc." Akbar took the disc out of his jacket, kissed it, then handed it to Ahmed.

"Guard this with your life, my friend. It's going to make us very wealthy in the end," Akbar reminded Ahmed.

"Will we make it to the end, my friend?"

"Yes, we will," Akbar replied.

"How long do you think that matter will take?" Ahmed inquired.

"It depends on how much we can trust the people involved. Then, I'm going to get back to other business," Akbar said. "Just stay alert and expect me to be getting back at you in several days. Make sure you put that disc in a safe place. It's our meal ticket."

The two men embraced once more, then entered their vehicles and headed in opposite directions with thoughts of a big payday in the immediate future.

Jaafar was across the street, seated behind tinted windows, taking pictures of Akbar and Ahmed. Tray had uncovered Akbar's whereabouts and had Jaafar monitoring his movements before he made the decision that would cost Akbar his life. Tray needed first to know who was involved, then the location of the disc or discs. Jaafar snapped pictures of Ahmed's license plate. That would lead him to the man's front door once the death warrant for his life was issued.

Seeing the two men end their discussion with an embrace and part ways, Jaafar slowly eased into traffic headed to New Orleans, cautiously stalking Akbar, monitoring the man's every movement, just like he had done many other men who were now pushing up daisies. He leaned back in his black Maserati. *In a matter of time, they'll be doing the same thing,* Jaafar thought.

Chapter 2

*R*ing, ring, ring . . .

James looked at his cell phone; it was a blocked number again. He quickly answered. "Hello?"

"Good morning," Tray responded.

"Good morning. What's going on?" James asked.

"Nothing much. Listen, I know this is sudden, and you probably have a full schedule. But can you get Troy and Deon together some time this morning? I want to meet with you all," Tray stated, anxiously awaiting the answer.

James paused a few seconds before answering. "You know it's Saturday, right?"

"I won't take up much of you guys' time."

Another pause of uncertainty from James followed. James knew this day would come. He just hadn't prepared for it, and that's what had him on edge. "Okay, we'll be at my office at 10:00 a.m."

"Perfect timing," Tray stated, then hung up.

James stood in the window overlooking Canal Street in a daze. He would finally get to see this man who had suddenly become instrumental in his business affairs. How did this person know so much about him and his family?

He simply didn't know where to begin asking questions, but he knew he needed answers. Perhaps the answers would be told without asking, James hoped.

Nevertheless, just in case dude was one of them crazy muthafuckas, James had artillery placed throughout the executive conference room. *He can fuck up if he wants to. It's going to be his birthday, real quick!*

"Knock, knock," Deon said as she and Troy strolled into the conference room, sporting sunglasses.

"Looks like some of us had a rough night," James suggested.

"Kinda sorta," Deon confessed.

"I'ma ridah," Troy stated, then leaned back in the comfortable chair. "They call these locs, and this is my bad boy look. However, Dee was out clubbing last night and probably had to be pried out of her bed."

"Yeah, right! For your information, I was halfway through a full workout when James called," Deon shot back, then rolled her eyes.

"All right, kids," James said. "The reason I asked you here is because our mystery caller wants to meet with us today, and he's on his way over now. Either of you have questions before he gets here?" James shifted his eyes between the two.

Deon and Troy looked at each other, then shook their heads.

"Naah," Troy said.

"We're sure you're going to cover all the bases," Deon commented.

James then changed the subject. "Have you two planned on watching any news today?" he asked.

"Do we need to, big brother?" Troy curiously asked.

"Well, today our little project will be broadcasted all over the world," James informed them.

"Yes yes yes! It's on now!" Troy jumped in the air with excitement.

Deon rushed over to James, then jumped into his arms. "I love you, I love you, I love you, big brother," she excitedly said. "You truly deserve this moment, James. It's your life's work!"

"Thanks, guys. This technology is as serious as cancer. I pray every day that it doesn't get us hurt—or worse. We have lived a nice life in many ways, but it pales in comparison to the immense wealth associated with this technology," James assured them.

"Man, we always been on top of our game in watching these fools out here," Troy said.

"No, Troy. I wish these street fools were who we're up against; they're the least of our worries."

"So, what exactly *are* we up against?" Deon asked.

"They are billionaires, Saudi princes, oil tycoons, people who have enough money to run entire countries. Their influence will attempt to derail our efforts to introduce our discoveries."

"So, we're going up against Big Government?" Deon inquired.

"Exactly," James stated. "They're going to throw the kitchen sink at us when this news gets out."

Beep, beep, beep.

"Yes, Janet," James answered the intercom.

"You have a visitor, Mr. Johnson."

"Send him up, Janet."

"We'll talk about this again soon. But you two promise me that you'll be attentive."

"You got that, big brother," Troy responded.

"I promise," Deon said with a smile.

Knock, knock.

"Come in," James stated.

Stepping through the door with briefcase in hand and powerful businessman written all over him, he greeted them. "Good morning," he said.

They were stunned as they all recognized him. It was Tray King, a longtime, close friend of the family.

"I haven't seen you since the funeral," James said.

"Neither have I," Deon stated.

"Right," Troy said.

"I know . . . my apologies. But just because you didn't see me doesn't mean that I wasn't there. I've been in your lives for longer than even you can remember. I just took the backseat. Troy, I was at your high school basketball games. I attended both your and Deon's graduations. I was also at your trial and sentencing. And I was the one who made the phone call after you left the courthouse.

"I remember that!" Deon expressed. "You left the envelope for James."

"That's right. James, I've watched over you in your rise to the top from day one. Remember when you just so happened to bump into this certain Cuban connect?"

"Who, Julio?" James questioned and stood up.

"That's right. He works for me. You were getting the best prices any man could've gotten at that time, without going to South America. Many men have secretly come up against you and died as a result."

"How do you know these things?" James inquired.

"Julio and the streets," Tray answered.

"Why did you not tell me? Why the secrecy?"

"First, I was your father's best friend, and for that reason, I was a part of your lives. However, your mother was a woman full of pride. I wanted to help her, but she would not accept a dime. She was truly independent, a real stand-up woman. So, I decided to help through you all. I figured the best way to help was to continue from behind the scenes. Then, once you started moving up in the game, I knew I had to stay out of the way. So, whoever came up against you would be fighting me too . . . which was a losing battle."

"You were that close to our family back then?" Troy asked.

"Me and your father were like Tom and Jerry." Tray smiled.

"My mother understood this, right?" Deon inquired.

"Yes, that's why she never took a dime from me. She thought your father ran off and was sending money through me."

"So, was she right?" James asked.

"She couldn't have been further from the truth."

"So where is he?" Deon asked.

"Truth is, I don't even know. But if I had to guess, I would say deceased."

"Why would you say that?" Troy asked.

"Because something happened before Wayne

disappeared, and we were the only ones who knew about it," Tray said.

"Would you care to share with us?" James asked.

Tray leaned back in the chair, then looked to the ceiling. He would finally open up about the incident that took place many years ago that he thought he'd have to take to the grave. He felt it was time Wayne's kids knew what really happened.

"One day, your father showed up with this kilo of cocaine and a story about how he'd stumbled upon a warehouse full of money and drugs. All he talked about is how he would buy his family a home and give them things they only wished they had. He bragged about your mother no longer having to work cleaning homes, and you three getting the best education money could buy. He would sneak in and out of the warehouse watching the Colombians come and go for an entire month. Then, we sprang into action with our plan. We pulled a moving truck into the warehouse and made off with millions of dollars in the safes we took, along with thousands of kilos. I later found out that a camera inside the warehouse was working on the backup power and had taped the entire caper. Your father was a big guy, so as he worked feverishly to empty the warehouse, he wiped his face, and his cap fell off. It exposed him to the camera taping the burglary. I was the only one who knew where everything was hidden besides him.

"We agreed not to touch anything until the time was right. Then, one day we were supposed to meet, and he never showed up. I knew he'd never miss our meeting without saying something. I didn't touch anything, just in case he needed to tell them where it was to save his life. But it was still there a month later and no sign of him; that could only mean one thing, logically."

Tray put his head down as the memories resurfaced.

"What could I tell your mother? I certainly couldn't tell her the truth. Even if I did, it would not have changed anything. At that point, I still had hope of him being alive. But," Tray said, snapping out of his emotional state, "even though he isn't here today, let me be a testimony of the love he held for his family."

Tray grabbed the briefcase, then placed it on the table. He retrieved the picture of him and Wayne and placed it on the table in front of James. He pointed to the picture, then stated, "He found something greater than himself . . . his family!"

James, Troy, and Deon were all in tears. All their lives they had been harboring nothing but resentment toward their father's memory. On a day when it should've been the happiest of their lives, it turned out to be the saddest.

Tray retrieved three folders, then handed one to each of them. The folders were financial portfolios. He had invested in various stocks and bonds for all three of them that were worth between sixty and seventy million each.

Troy whistled. "All this for me?"

"Yes, it has grown quite a bit since it was opened," Tray said.

"Damn, man. You and daddy must've been cooler than the other side of the pillow," Troy guessed.

"Man, you don't know the half. Your father was my

best friend; he was who I wanted to be. He was a hustler because nobody would give him a chance out here. He'd rather hustle than let one of them crackers shine on him for a couple of nickels, and work him like a runaway slave for it. I always knew he'd get that big lick he talked so much about, but I never thought that he wouldn't be here to enjoy it. I've raised two beautiful children and gave them lives they never had coming if it wasn't for Wayne. Who I am, and what you see and hear is because of your father. I don't know what you plan to do with this information, but I love you all like my very own. I would like nothing more than for our relationship to continue. That's why I asked to meet today."

James stood, then reached for Tray's hand. They shook hands, and James pulled him forward. Troy and Deon joined in the embrace. Silently, the siblings wept for different reasons, but mostly for the torment they were forced to live through and forever awaken to. Besides being siblings, there was something else they shared. Yet, they could never muster the strength to share that with each other. How could they feel comfortable in doing so? Life had forced them to leap over a traditional childhood. Reality had snatched away the trial and error teachings they were supposed to experience through their adolescent years. Fate would ultimately decide they'd grow up without their loving parents. But faith gave them the strength to endure. And now, God had sent them an angel. Tray had been there all along. Now, they all hugged him tightly, releasing a plethora of tears, reminders of the hurt and pain of their brutal past. Yes, they were still broken, and perhaps one day they'd speak of it. But that day was a long way off. And perhaps more importantly, they found solace in navigating others like them away from this torment.

Chapter 3

"*I'm Wolf Blitzer at CNN News, and you're in the Situation Room.*" The music began playing in the background as the show was about to air.

"*Today, there are reports of new groundbreaking discoveries of alternative fuel for cars that are essentially made from cocaine and heroin. We're joined here today by a scientist who claims he is one of three scientists who developed this latest technology, Doctor Chowu. Doctor, can you tell our viewers how this research came about?*"

"*Basically, two of my colleagues and I received a call from a gentleman that had an idea of turning something bad in our society into something good for our society.*"

"*So, the basis of the research isn't for profit?*" Wolf asked.

"*From day one, this project has been centered around the adverse effects drugs are having on our society. This made me more accepting of the challenge. We knew it would be an uphill battle, but that's our life's dedication. Science is what our professions are all about, and we viewed this project as a good cause, win, lose, or draw,*" Doctor Chowu stated.

"*So, how do you get the vehicles of today to run off this new fuel?*"

"*They won't. There are three scientists, as I have stated. I created the chemical portion, Doctor Sanja created the brain, or the computer chip portion, and Doctor Gore created the engine that runs off the other technologies. What we have done, as a whole, is built a vehicle that generates electricity. It's an electronic car that charges its battery."*

"So, there's no reason to stop and plug the battery up like the electric cars manufactured today?" Wolf inquired.

"Not anymore. Also, these new vehicles have little or no effect on the environment. The fuel is clean, and a tank of fuel will last your average American a month."

"Wow! That's definitely going to send oil producers into a tailspin. How exactly will this latest technology work when assembled together?" Wolf inquired.

"As I've stated, the cars will be electric. So, they will run totally off the battery. Doctor Sanja, a world-renowned neurologist, duplicated the portion of the brain that triggers addiction. As we know, when people do drugs, they become addicted. So the computer chip is then made part of the fuel tank. And, if fuel is present, a continual signal will be sent to the engine. The engine design is similar to a power plant. It generates its own electricity as the signal from the chip turns the magnet, creating friction that sends negative and positive electrons to the battery continuously."

"How long has this research been going on?" Wolf asked.

"About five years."

"And when should we expect to see the vehicles of the future?"

"Possibly three to six months, as I understand. The factories are being built here and abroad as we speak."

"So, this technology won't just benefit America?"

"Oh no. This has to benefit other countries too because it takes from those countries. Drug smuggling and the manufacturing of these drugs are these countries' economy. The

gentleman behind this idea has made it a global benefit. The drug lords can sell their drugs to this company, which are turned into fuel at the factories being built. We're creating a drug-free society here. So, there will be no more drug smuggling. They can now help their economy with the jobs the factories create, and less money spent by their governments toward a war against drugs," Doctor Chowu stated.

"That's fascinating information, but we're almost out of time. I want to thank you for coming today and sharing this truly astonishing news. Can you possibly tell our viewers the name of the gentleman responsible for this monumental accomplishment?"

"Not a chance. I'll leave that up to him," Doctor Chowu responded.

Minutes later, telephone calls were being placed from all corners of the globe, wondering if this rumor was for real.

Billionaires were calling their contacts to lobby against this latest technology. There would be trillions of dollars lost for the oil industry if this technology was real, Fox News reported.

"Over my dead body!" an oil tycoon stated in his blog.

"Who dat muthafucka?" Kane yelled at the Atlanta fans that were in the skybox seats at the Georgia Dome.

The Atlanta Falcons were winning the first half when Drew Brees and Michael Thomas went to work. Kane and Diamond were decked out in their Saints gear from head to toe. The Falcons' fans were driving them hard the first half; now it was payback. Kane started chunking back shots of Hennessy like it was his birthday. The more he drank, the more he bet.

"You muthafuckas still wanna bet?" Kane shouted.

J-Rock, a grand hustler from Atlanta, stood up. "Yeah, nigga. You make the call!"

"He must think he talking to a broke nigga," Kane said to Diamond with a smile.

"What did you drive here, homie?" Kane inquired.

"An S65 AMG Mercedes. You got one?"

"No, but I will. Bet that!" Kane boasted. "How much did that car cost you?"

"A hundred grand or so. You got that?" J-Rock asked.

"It just so happens, I carry about that much around." Kane slung his dreads to the back and put a band on them, then started reaching deep into his jeans pocket.

Everything got quiet as J-Rock and his dude, Chaz, leaned back and listened to Kane count out the money.

"Eighty-five, eighty-six, eighty-seven, eighty-eight, eighty-nine, ninety thousand."

"Diamond, count me out another ten grand, baby," Kane said. "And I'm even going to throw in a little extra for you other non-Saints lovers." Kane counted out another twenty-nine grand. "Shit, I may have to quit my day job and start traveling with the Saints. By the way, you sure you can bet that Mercedes, or is it for the wife?"

"I don't keep none of them around; I'm married to my work. But that's a bet, homeboy. You still down by three in this game," J-Rock added.

"Shiiid, that's nothing compared to what you're

going to be down, my brother. Just sit back and enjoy the show."

Kane's dude, C-Black, was kicked back, but so was his new recruit for one of his strip clubs. His wife wasn't fond of football games, so C-Black took full advantage. He was also tossing back shots, enjoying the show Kane was putting on.

Drew Brees slung a touchdown to Alvin Kamari for forty yards at the end of the quarter. The fourth quarter ended with Atlanta driving eighty yards, but failed to get into the end zone on three tries, settling for a field goal. The score was now 30-29, Saints' way.

"Taking all bets!" Kane shouted. "This is where we pull off from you boys. Hey, homie, you got a ride home?"

"Yeah, if I need one. I got a helicopter too. You got one of those?"

"Not unless you're willing to bet the one you flying around town," Kane said, laughing, and so did everyone else.

C-Black knew J-Rock was getting heated because J-Rock never was another nigga's joke. He and his dude, Chaz, were killers when it came down to it. Kane was accumulating the wrong type of publicity. C-Black knew he'd have to pull Kane's coat after the game once the alcohol wore off.

Kane looked back at C-Black and winked as the time ticked off the clock. The Saints now led by fifteen, with two minutes left. J-Rock and Chaz sat there steaming but had to respect the game. Kane strolled over to the table where the stacks of money and keys were. He started picking up the money, stuffing it into his pockets. The clock read double zero, and the people began leaving. Kane picked up the keys, then walked over to J-Rock and Chaz.

He tossed the keys to J-Rock, then stated, "The name is Kane, and I never wanted one of them, anyway! But this is what's up, homie. I'm new around here and don't know my way around yet. I do my own thing in my own way, but I dig real niggas in big ways. Material shit don't excite me. I get money. Like I said, I'm new, and looking for some real niggas to shoot some marbles with. Y'all know C-Black. He can give you the history of my struggles in this game, from the beginning to the end. I don't need your car or helicopter." Kane cracked a smile. "I could use your alliance, though."

"I hear you talking, homeboy. And if you know C-Black, then you know who I am. But you won that vehicle like a man, and that's the only way I know how to get down. It wasn't gon' be no big deal because I was absorbing your style, and I respected how you came. Shit, I'm always hoping to run into niggas like us that ain't afraid to lose. Niggas like you keep my game sharp. It's all about growth, homeboy. Take my number and give me a holla with what you have on your brain, then we can see if we can put it in motion, and take it there."

"Fo' sho'," Kane stated.

Everybody shook hands, then went their separate ways. Kane walked away, thinking about putting a team together, then heading back to New Orleans, causing hell. He knew many hungry goons were in Atlanta looking for a payday, as well as wanting to make a name for themselves. The idea of them fighting against the nigga James, who was threatening the drug game, would be an honor.

At 12:00 p.m. on a beautiful Sunday in Cancún, Mexico, George McNamara, Rafael Fernandez, and Pablo Hernandez were out boating. The clear blue waters sparkled as the sunlight danced on top of it. The men lay back drinking champagne and speaking about their plan to get rid of President Malik Quinn. George was chugging back glasses of alcohol as if it were his birthday. Pablo and Rafael kept pouring shots like bartenders. George, over an hour, made three trips to the restroom. The last trip he wobbled the entire way, bumping and falling into every wall he approached.

"Sit down, George," Pablo said as George made it back from the restroom once more.

George complied, feeling the effects of the expensive bourbon.

"What's up, Pablo?" he asked.

"My friend," Pablo began, "we have accomplished many things over two decades through your political connections in the United States and abroad."

"You're damn right we did," George agreed in his slurred speech. "And we're not finished!" he added, waving a finger in Pablo's direction.

"However, this latest plan has not been what I've expected of you, my friend. It has taken entirely too much time and resources to pull off," Pablo stated.

"Goddammit, be patient, you son of a bitch," George shouted drunkenly.

"No, my friend. Patience has allowed me to be exposed to a very powerful person, and it is all because of your patience! This time, I'll take care of the problem without patience," Pablo insisted.

"What the fuck are you talking about? You doubt me, after all the money I've put into your pockets? You doubt me, you low-life fuckin' drug dealer?" George yelled while attempting to get up, but he fell back on wobbly legs.

"Calm down, George," Rafael stated.

"Fuck you too, Rafael!"

"No muthafucka, fuck you!" Rafael shot back.

"George, you're right about the low-life drug dealer you called me. However, you couldn't have picked a worst time to speak your true feelings. It is said that a drunkard will tell you their true feelings without fail. Thank you, George. Now, I won't feel so bad about killing you today," Pablo declared.

"What do you mean, *killing me today*?" George stated, as his entire complexion changed.

"That's right, George. You will die today. This most likely never crossed your mind at any point today . . . until now," Rafael stated. "But it is the God honest truth; your end is here."

"But-but why?" George was stunned by the revelation.

"Well, it's either you or us," Rafael stated plainly.

"What do you mean?"

"What I mean is that James Johnson returned our

ten-million-dollar investment to us that we gave to you. And since we're nothing but low-life drug dealers, we possess no loyalty to anything but ourselves and our money. Mr. Johnson has offered us both," Rafael stated with raised eyebrows.

"But why me? Why fuck up a good thing?" George reasoned.

"Why you?" Pablo questioned while laughing. "You're a man that has killed and destroyed the lives of a multitude of people in your rise to fame, and you ask *why you?*"

"Yes, I asked why me, motherfucker!" George shouted.

"Let's just call it Karma." Rafael and Pablo rose, then took hold of George and violently threw him overboard, knowing he couldn't swim.

Their women were still ashore, preparing dinner when they received the call that George had fallen overboard, and instantly went under. The Coast Guard was called to the scene in minutes. An hour later, they pulled George's lifeless body from beneath the waters of the Gulf of Mexico. Apparently, he stumbled and fell on the boat. He'd hit his head trying to gain his balance, then went overboard. Neither Pablo nor Rafael knew how to swim, and neither had life vests. The Coast Guard ticketed both of them. The authorities notified the White House; then President Malik held a press conference.

"Today, we lost a very dear friend in a boating accident while on vacation in Cancún, Mexico. George McNamara was my top advisor and the primary reason today I stand before

you as your commander in chief. He will be sorely missed, and my thoughts and prayers go out to his family and friends," President Malik Quinn stated during the press conference.

James was watching the broadcast along with Tray at his mansion in Slidell. The two men had talked about so much business and personal affairs over the brief time they were together; both were fascinated by the other's stories. James really enjoyed having Tray around for his wisdom and advice. He confided in Tray about the George situation, and Tray understood the politics involved, then agreed that George's days were numbered no matter what.

"You're just like your father, James," Tray complimented him.

"In what way would that be?"

"He was a shrewd thinker. I called him 'The Fixer.' Wayne had the patience of a snail. Like when he stumbled upon that lick, his idea worked. He timed it perfectly. Shit, after he told me about it, I was ready to get what I could right then and there. You see, Wayne understood that the Colombians had been there a minute and the operation was too sweet to mess up and move because they were paranoid. Nobody knew about it but those in that circle, and they weren't telling a soul," Tray said.

"Hey, what do you think about me going on *The Oprah Show*?"

"You're the one with the big ideas. Embrace it; it's your destiny. Your life depends on it. The world will be watching you, wanting in many ways to be you! True success is measured by the lives you've affected in a lifetime. This separates you from many other great people. The success of your idea is immeasurable; the mark of a true visionary."

"Thanks, Tray. This is very reassuring. It does seem like we've come far; then it seems like we have so far to go. I mean, we actually have a black president now. That is very significant. Then, on the other hand, you got those rich white and black folks that don't want things ever to change. They're going to fight what's right every step of the way," James said.

"It's a cruel world we're living in, mainly because we're living amongst cruel people. You're an exception to the status quo. You must continue. We must continue doing what we have to do. You and Malik have that stage you set out to build. Let's keep on adding to it, no matter the obstacles. Because nothing can stop the man with the right mental attitude from achieving his goal, and nothing can help the man with the wrong mental attitude."

Three Saudi princes were walking through the palace of King Shalik Khalid. The palace was enormous and beautifully decorated. The floors, walls, and ceiling were made of multicolored marble. Ancient artifacts lined the hallways, along with lavish furniture. The palace was more like a museum than a home. The servant escorted the three men to King Khalid's office.

"Please be seated, gentlemen," King Khalid said. "I

called you here today because of a very pressing matter that's threatening the business we're controlling." The three men nodded in agreement, knowing the king's concerns.

"I think all of you are aware of these latest developments concerning this 'alternative' fuel, right?" The men nodded once more.

"Plain and simple, we can't just sit around and wait for our product to become obsolete. Something drastic has to be done!"

"What can we do if this new fuel has already been created, then approved?" Prince Abdullah asked.

"We can wage war against the people attempting to introduce this new technology," King Khalid stated. "We have enough money and resources to fight this until the end of time!"

"However, what if it's what the people want?" Prince Zamir asked. "Furthermore, I think the people are sold on the implications of what the new technology brings to the table."

"What do they know, other than what's being reported, that this new technology will supposedly do? Who knows for sure?" King Khalid said.

"The scientists seem to know for sure," Prince Ahrah stated. "Who can argue with science? Whoever is behind this idea, quieted all the potential critics by allowing the scientists to unveil the discovery. It was a brilliant plan. I'm anxious to meet this individual."

"Fuck this individual!" King Khalid expressed. "He's

attempting to take money out of my pocket. That's all *I* need to know about him!"

"I think what the strategy should be may not have much to do with war as it would be to obtain somehow the ingredients they'll need to manufacture this fuel," Prince Ahrah responded. "If we could purchase the drugs at a price that can't be matched, then it shuts down their distribution of the fuel, and that means no new vehicles."

"How about we do both?" King Khalid suggested. "There obviously is someone real damn smart behind this idea, so we'll cut off the head; then the body will fall!"

"Now we're making sense. A little bit of both should slow this thing down for sure. Now, let's agree on what countries to visit, then spread a little money around. Everyone loves money," Prince Abdullah added.

"We certainly have our work cut out for us. My guess is whoever is behind this idea has gone where we're about to go, and he proposed unbelievable prices to buy the drugs produced in those countries. So, we'll have to do better than he did. It's the American way," King Khalid said.

"As a final thought, men, we have the world eating out of our hand right now. Someone is trying to move our hand and replace it with theirs. Whenever I find out who these people are, we'll have a team of assassins at their home in the blink of an eye. Do you all agree to that assessment of this current problem?" the king asked.

The princes nodded; then they all began to leave the

palace en route to their next destination, which was to convince the drug lords to deal with them instead. If only the king and princes had the gift of foresight . . . They would've stayed home.

Chapter 4

"Hello, everybody. A month ago, world-renowned scientist, Dr. J. Chowu made an appearance on CNN's, The Situation Room *with Wolfe Blitzer to talk about their groundbreaking discovery. We're joined here today on* The Oprah Show *for an exclusive interview with the man behind the vision. So give him a round of applause, everyone, introducing businessman, lawyer, and entrepreneur, Mr. James Johnson! This gentleman has caused an uproar all over the world concerning his brilliant idea that began over five years ago,"* Oprah explained.

The audience began applauding at the sight of James seated opposite Oprah in a brown pin-striped Armani suit, looking like a billionaire.

"Mr. Johnson, what did you think when this idea came about five years ago?"

"Basically, I realized something the government seemed always to want to hide."

"What's that?" Oprah inquired.

"That drugs are the number one reason we have such a huge disconnect within black communities," James replied.

"So, what do you suggest they do, Mr. Johnson?"

"What they will never do. Stop the drugs from coming here in the first place."

"Aha. Do you think the government can stop the drugs from entering the United States?" Oprah curiously asked.

"Certainly, if they wanted to. They're the reason why drugs are here now. Why would they not know how to stop it?" James asked.

"That's a good question, Mr. Johnson."

"It's doing just what it's designed to do, and to who it's designed to do it to. They call it genocide. Drug use leads to crimes that lead to the imprisoning of our potential black leaders of the future. The government would rather see these men and women behind bars, than behind conglomerate companies providing the landscape for the next generation coming after them. The government will pay three times the amount to incarcerate, rather than send that person to a prestigious college," James stated as a matter of fact.

"So, you think it would be a better investment to educate than to incarcerate?"

"Most definitely. You send these men and women to get educated, they become independent, taxpaying, productive citizens. You send them to prison, and they're around more criminals. That enables them to learn to become a better criminal and a greater problem once their time is up. You throw away the key. Then, the taxpayers must take care of these individuals for the rest of their lives. The rising health care of the older offenders are doubling, and even tripling the cost of your average offenders, who are less of a threat. The present system isn't a solution; it's the problem. Drugs are the problem, not the people that use them. Just as guns don't kill people. People with guns kill people," James said.

"So, what would be a short- and long-term solution?" Oprah asked.

"The first step would be to eliminate the drugs. Step two

*would be preventing the next generation from adapting crimi-
nalistic values by incorporating new programs that prepare
these young people for the future. Instead of your children de-
fining what's relevant by associating it only with what's going
on in the hood, while the rest of the world educates their kids
about the future, we teach them to look beyond the hood."*

*"Let's talk about what this discovery will do for these
causes," Oprah stated, while crossing her legs, then placing
her hands on her lap.*

*"First of all, our communities will no longer have to look
for governments to educate them for the future. I'm bringing
the future to them. The new technologies associated with my in-
ventions will be taught in schools I'm building throughout urban America. If someone successfully completes these schools,
there will be a six-figure job waiting for them with opportunities to buy stock in my company. I've secured contracts with
all the drug lords in every country known to smuggle drugs
into the United States. The drugs will only be sold to Johnson
Industries. I am doing what the government could've done a
long time ago, but too much power and money are changing
hands with politicians. With me, it's not about power and money; I don't want their money nor power. I want my people,"
James aggressively stated.*

*"To my understanding, your technologies will not just
help African Americans, but the world in general."*

*"Yes, Oprah. That's true. You eliminate a lot of negative
elements when drugs become extinct. Plus, the job creation will
be dramatic because of the factories I'll build in addition to the
schools. The factories will be built all over the world benefiting
all countries and all people."*

"So, what about the millions of Americans employed at the plants for Ford, GM, Chrysler, and the rest?" Oprah inquired.

"They all could still exist; there is just going to be a new dealer on the block," James said, smiling.

"But, how can they compete with your product when you outperform them in every aspect?"

"I think they'll survive. There's always constant change in America. They'll come up with something down the line, or they can come work for me," James stated, then winked at Oprah as the show concluded.

Keoka was at her boutique in the Eastern New Orleans, kickin' it with her girl, Juicy-J, while doing inventory. Juicy-J was one of Kane's women before he went to the penitentiary. She was real pissed off when Kane left. They had planned on going to Houston and catching the R&B tour featuring R. Kelly, Keyshia Cole, and J. Holiday. Kane had been gone a minute, but she still was bitter. Keoka, being the investigator she is, decided to offer information to gain a little hopefully.

"Girl, you ain't heard this from me, but you know you my girl. Shit, they got some bitch talking about she carrying Kane's baby."

"What? Girl, you got to be bullshitting me!" Juicy-J said as she spun around from the clearance rack of clothing that she was picking through.

"No, girl. You know I ain't going to bring no bad meat to the table," Keoka continued.

"That low-down muthafucka! He around here naked

heading these hoes out here, enough to kill a bitch on the cool. That's fucked up!" Juicy-J stated.

"Girl, that nigga ain't holla at you yet?" Keoka asked, knowing he hadn't.

"No, girl. His jive ass never said shit, not even when he left."

"Girl, I miss his crazy ass too," Keoka said. "If he holla, which he will, just give him time. But tell him I said to keep his head up."

"You know you my girl. I gots to lace you up, 'cause that nigga will miss jumping in between these legs, He'll surface, baby. He always does. Girl, was you at Club Ballers the other night?"

"You already know, shit was off the hook with all them stars in that bitch. Looked like we was in a planetarium or something," Keoka stated. "For them hundred dollars at the door, I had a handful of Jeezy's ass!"

"Yo' ass is too damn bold. Enough for one of them bodyguard niggas to lay yo' ass down."

"I wish he would've tried. I would've cut his ass everywhere he had an artery pumping blood," Keoka assured her.

"Damn, girl, who are those fine-ass niggas coming in here?" Juicy-J asked.

"Oh, that's Dip and Jon-Jon, girl. Them my peeps," Keoka said as she looked up from stacking jeans on shelves.

"What's up Keoka, baby?" Dip inquired.

"A bitch still trying to stay out of the welfare line, big brother. What's cracking? I know yo' li'l stanky ass ain't acting funny, huh, Jon-Jon?"

"No, indeed not, dark and lovely. I was just lost in a fantasy, looking at this ebony showcase fashion model you failed to introduce us to."

Keoka looked around the store for whomever Jon-Jon was talking about, then her eyes landed on Juicy-J.

"That bitch ain't no model; that's Juicy-J, boy."

"She Juicy-J to you, but she an Ebony model to me," Jon-Jon said.

"Stop hating, Keoka, with yo' black ass!" Juicy-J shouted.

"Chocolate to you, ho," Keoka responded.

Juicy-J looked Jon-Jon up and down. She licked her lips, giving him a seal of approval.

"Ummm, let's get from around all this traffic. Bye, hater," Juicy-J stated with her middle finger pointed at Keoka.

"Bye, tramp. I mean slut!"

"Look here, Dip," Keoka whispered. "I was just tryin' a get info outta that bitch. That's one of Kane's bitches."

"Oh yeah?"

"I'm on my shit, nigga." Keoka gave Dip a high five.

"So, what she had to say?" Dip inquired as he peeped around, then leaned into Keoka's space.

"Shit, the nigga ain't got at her yet. She fuming too. Acting like she his wifey." Keoka rolled her eyes at the insanity of Juicy-J's simplemindedness.

"Dat nigga Kane played her ass like everyone else, huh?" Dip asked.

"That's right. Now his ass running for his life," she said, walking to the front of the store.

"Well, if you should hear anything else, give me a call."

"Will do. As soon as he contacts any of his hoes, I'll be the first they'll come gossip to," she laughed.

"And you'll be rewarded," Dip reminded her, as he looked around the store.

"Shit, I'm good," Keoka stated, waving her hand around as if she were showcasing her high-end clothing and accessory boutique on the *Price Is Right*.

"I see that. Looks like you have a lot of square footage too."

"That ain't all I have either." She ushered him to the back of the store, where she navigated through the racks and shelves of clothing and many accessories.

"Where the hell you taking me?" Dip asked.

"Shut up, nigga. I'm trying to put you up on something!" She stopped momentarily, peeping toward the front of the store, looking to see if Juicy-J and Jon-Jon were still outside. She took a few more steps and rounded a corner that ended at an office door with a camera lodged in the right upper corner of the ceiling and wall. There was a keypad just below the handle. Keoka tapped in the code, and a double chirp sounded off. She pulled down the handle, grabbed his arm, pulled him into the room, then closed the door behind them.

The moment Dip entered the room, he stood in awe. It was the size of a regular bedroom. The walls were black as well as the ceiling and black marble floors. Keoka strolled around a massive antique black and gold desk that rested atop a beautifully crafted black and gold embroidered Turkish rug. Then she took a seat and studied Dip.

The back wall was a bookshelf that held hundreds of books. The other three walls held paintings, all signifying social issues of the past, present, and future. Yet, they weren't pictures; they were statements and slogans that asked questions like: "Equality in America is a Right, right?" or "Social Justice, is it still justice, or is it still just-us?"

Dip was captivated by the overall feel of the room. The sheer design gave the notion that it was telling you something, just as Keoka had said, *"I'm trying to put you up on something."* He looked at Keoka, puzzled. Wrinkles lined his forehead as he gave her a side-eyed look. Then he walked in a circular motion around her massive desk. She was smiling. Yet, it appeared that another Keoka had replaced the old one. Her facial expression now held a different demeanor, as if it were a mask. Intense, intelligent, and calculated was this Keoka.

He turned away in an attempt to get a read on her thoughts, then in the corner stood another painting. A huge, gallery-wrapped one that stood about five feet by five feet. A black background with random bright pastel-colored letters made the statement: "I am a Man! A Great Man!! A Wise Man!!! A Black Man!!!! Man!!!!!"

Dip studied the painting, stroking his chin. Then he slowly did a 360, stopped at a high-tech computer system with six full-screen monitors that not only showed the inside and outside of the boutique, but the surrounding area, neighborhoods, as well as the interstates. He walked around to the front of Keoka's desk, sat down in one of the two chairs in front, then asked, "Who the fuck are you?"

Keoka leaned back in the comfortable brown leather chair, then gave a devilish grin.

FBI Agent John Cage was seated behind his desk, viewing the TV screen as James finished his interview on *The Oprah Show*. The smirk on John's face said that he wouldn't rest until he locked James and his organization away for life. He had developed a hatred for him and his family. There was no doubt in his mind from the extensive investigation of the killings that were happening in Jefferson Parish that James, Luqman, and Troy were behind them.

John had authorized agents to monitor different stores and offices of Luqman's businesses and where two agents were killed in an explosion triggered by a car bomb. John couldn't explain the sightings of possible Taliban around those areas, but now he knew why they were here. John had wanted to get a glimpse of who this man was, and was now impressed by what he'd seen and heard. He knew this man would be a major problem. In a room filled with geniuses, James would no doubt appear to be the smartest. At that moment, John wondered if he would ever get close enough to this man to build a case against him. His mind reminisced about the shootings that happened on the courthouse steps in Jefferson Parish, and he concluded that they were being toyed with. James and his organization were steps ahead of him and his people. *But all I need is a break,* John thought.

"Excuse me, sir." The switchboard officer interrupted John over the intercom in his office, as she watched him ignore her transfer of a call from her desk.

"Yes," John replied, snapping out of his daydream.

"You have a call from Washington on line seven."

"Thank you," John stated.

"John Cage speaking."

"John, this is Mike Brown. How are you doing down there in the Crescent City?"

"Oh, hey, Mike. I'm okay, I guess. Another day, another dime. More or less the same ol' shit. What's up?"

"I may have stumbled upon something you might need in a future case."

"Oh yeah? Which one is that?" John asked.

"James Johnson."

John almost dropped the telephone at the mention of James's name.

"You still there, John?"

"Yeah. I'm still here, Mike. What's this something?"

"I need to dot my i's and cross my t's on this individual, but one of my informants have a thing for this guy and wants to bring him down in a major way. I heard you were on a case down there, and every little bit helps in our field. I'm planning a trip down that way soon. We'll get together and go over what we have. Cool?" Mike asked.

"That's great, Mike. And thanks, buddy. I could use some news, considering the drama down here," John admitted.

"Talk to you again soon, John." Then the phone went dead.

Immediately John's phone began to ring.

"Hello?" he answered on the third ring.

"John, this is Agent Averez. I've been staking out the store in Gentilly, and I know this area and people very well."

"So, what's the problem, Agent Averez?"

"Sir, there looks to be a sudden surge of foreigners in and out of the stores. It just seems unusual. I was thinking about the explosives used on the agents' car, and now the foreigners pop up. Do you believe in coincidences?"

"Not really. But you stay out of sight and document all that in your report. We'll discuss it later."

"Will do, sir. Just thought you needed to know," Agent Averez stated, then hung up the phone.

Quickly, John made a call.

"Agent Holloway speaking."

"Agent, this is John Cage. Are you still on duty surveying the store on Martin Luther King Boulevard?"

"Yes sir."

"Did you see anything unusual up there?"

"Not really; normal activities."

"Do you see a few more than the usual number of foreigners at that store?"

"No more than usual, sir."

"How many would that be?"

"About four or five. They seem to work there."

"Why do you say that?"

"Because they're always discussing Luqman or Troy, and sometimes they leave with them."

"Thanks, Agent. Keep up the good work." John Cage now needed to find out exactly where these foreigners were coming from. *Maybe I can tie James into some terrorist organizations too,* he thought.

Chapter 5

"Surprise!" everyone yelled as James entered his mansion in Slidell. After *The Oprah Show,* he hung out in Los Angeles awhile before heading back to Louisiana. The show went well. Everybody wanted to shake his hand and ask more questions, especially about how they could sign up for James's schools.

Troy, Deon, Tray, Jaafar, Luqman, and Salvator were at the mansion laughing and joking and having a good time. Then suddenly, Troy's phone rang.

"Hello?" he answered.

"Hey, we're at the front gate. Can you let these goons know who we are?" Tysha stated. Troy had met her and her friend Joy at Club Ballers and later introduced them to Deon, and the women cliqued instantly.

"Hand Bruno the phone," Troy replied.

"What's up?" the 300-pound ex-linebacker said into the phone.

"They're cool, Bruno. Let them up," Troy stated. He invited both women to the party because they were respectable and nothing like many of the loose women that frequented the nightclub circuit. Joy was a professor at Tulane University, and Tysha was an executive for a security firm. But more importantly, he was really digging Tysha. He wanted to get to know her in a better setting. Plus, he figured that Joy was James's type.

"Okay, Troy," he replied, handing the phone back to Tysha.

Tysha put the phone back to her ear. "Troy?"

"Everything is all good now, right?" Troy inquired. He was thinking about the huge Jacuzzi in the backyard. He had his mind set on skinny-dipping. "You got your swimsuit, right?"

"Now, why would I not, Troy?" she questioned.

"Just checking, baby."

"Whatever, Troy with yo' li'l nasty self. Open the door; we've made it."

Troy opened the door, then Tysha and Joy strolled into the mansion.

"Damn, this is a really nice home," Tysha stated.

"Hello, ladies, I'm James. Welcome to my home. A friend of my brother or sister is a friend of mine."

"Oh, yeah, James. This is Joy, whom I was telling you about. She and Tysha are originally from Atlanta but recently moved here to LA," Troy stated.

"Nice to meet you two. Can I get you ladies something to drink?" James asked, looking Joy over extensively. She blushed.

"I could use a—"

James held up his hand, pausing Tysha, then snapped his fingers, getting the waiter's attention. The waiter hurried toward him.

"Lionel, can you please get these ladies a drink?"

"No problem, sir."

"Let me know if there's anything else you ladies need," James offered.

Troy engaged the women in conversation but smirked once he saw Joy's eyes following James as he walked away.

James walked toward Tray, Salvator, and Jaafar, who were all standing around the room.

"I don't think I've met you, Mister . . ." Salvator said.

"Jaafar," came the reply as the two men shook hands.

"We are what you might say, cut from the same cloth," Salvator stated, then winked at Tray.

James looked at the two men, then at Tray and figured something else wasn't being said. Tray stood there with his arms spread out. James shook his head.

"I need a drink," James commented.

"Me too," said Tray.

The night was moving along perfectly. James was totally engaged in conversation with Joy. Chances were slim that she would be going home tonight. Everybody was cutting the rug on the dance floor with the smooth sounds of Miguel blaring from the state-of-the-art sound system installed into the mansion's ballroom. "Why I Love You" was being sung by everyone as the song's lyrics made them reminisce on their earlier years.

The strangest feeling hit James, disrupting his conversation with Joy. He reminded himself that everything was moving along perfectly, and he'd enjoy this night by continuing to converse with this beautiful woman.

"Am I talking too much about my profession?" Joy asked. "You seem distracted."

"No, no. Not at all. My mind is always on the go. It's nothing," he lied.

Troy and Tysha ended their dance and walked out back to begin their lovemaking session. Troy was seated in a lounge chair while Tysha danced around the patio, high on expensive champagne and Cognac. Troy thought he'd seen some movement in the corner. He never stopped watching her dance, but he was now on high alert.

"Why are you looking at me all crazy like that?" Tysha asked.

Suddenly, Troy saw more movement but knew what time of day it was. He wanted to run and try to save Tysha at the end of the patio, but he knew it would've cost him his life. His next thought was to get back into the house and alert everyone. He made his move, rolling out of the lounge chair and continuing to roll without attempting to get up. Suddenly, gunfire filled the air as the glass doors shattered.

Braca, braca, braca, tat, tat, tat.

Then a whistling sound sailed through the air, accompanied by a huge explosion. Whatever it was landed in the kitchen. Troy made it inside as he slipped and dodged the assassins' bullets. He looked back for a second, only to see Tysha's lifeless body lying out on the patio.

Troy turned the corner, seeing everybody running for cover. Nobody had weapons on them, so he had to take the chance and get to the bookshelf. He and James were the only ones who knew about the weapons room and which book to pull to activate the secret entrance. James was out of position as he made eye contact with Troy, knowing he was thinking the same thing. Troy maneuvered through the house until he reached the book, pulled it, and the room opened up. The whistling sounds continued, followed by more explosions as if it were the Gulf War! Troy was sliding weapons out of the room and passing them to Luqman, Jaafar, Salvator, Tray, and James. Gunfire was all around them.

Pop, pop, tat, tat.

They started hitting back.

Tat, tat, tat, braca, braca, braca.

"I'm hit!" Troy screamed in pain.

"Stay down!" Jaafar shouted.

Salvator and Jaafar slid on the floor through the glass like experts. They went through the broken glass, leaving bloody trails as they went in search of assassins.

Tray had managed to get back to the weapons room after running out of ammunition. Now, he was holding two AK-47s. Suddenly, the front door came crashing down, then the whistling sounds followed. Screams now followed the explosions. Two men with weapons stepped through.

On their blindside, Tray stood with both AKs strapped to each shoulder, firing the guns as if he were a madman on a mission. The two assassins never saw it coming. Portions of the house were ablaze, and the fire was spreading. Tray left the two dead assassins in search of more to kill. Fewer gunshots were now heard. The men were pulling out. Jaafar and Salvator had managed to sneak down on at least ten of them. *Fucking amateurs!* they thought.

Sirens were heard from miles away as the neighbors had reported gunfire and the mansion on fire. The mansion was destroyed. Troy ran back into the house, looking for everyone to see who else was hurt. He began calling names.

"Deon! James!" he called, but there was no answer. "Everybody okay?" he asked.

"I'm okay," Joy stated. She was sniffling at the sight of her friend, Tysha.

"Anybody seen James or Deon?" Troy asked.

Tray walked around with the AKs still strapped to him. His face was twisted like a soldier still trapped in Vietnam. He dropped the guns, then started turning over furniture, looking for James and Deon. He then made his way to the bar, where he saw James's legs sticking out. He flipped the minibar off James, and Deon lay underneath James. He was covering her, and they both were wounded.

A caravan of police and fire trucks made their way to the front gates. The two guards were found slumped on the floor with bullet holes in their head.

"Open the gates!" the commander stated to the officer who discovered the bodies.

The gate retracted, then the convoy entered the premises of what was left of James's mansion. Once up the hill, the paramedics, firefighters, and police began jumping out of their vehicles with haste.

"No no no. This can't be!" Troy stated. "Not now! Why did this have to happen to us, man? They can't be gone. What will I do now? What the fuck am I going to do now?" Troy was frantically pacing the floor.

"Sir, are you hurt?" the female paramedic asked him.

He didn't even hear her. He continued walking in circles, saying the same things.

The paramedics quickly strapped Deon and James to a gurney and headed to the hospital.

"Where's Luqman?" Troy asked Jaafar.

"He was found out back, but he's alive. They took him to the hospital too."

"Man, what am I gonna do, huh?"

"You're going to go on—win, lose, or draw. That's what the strong do," Tray said.

"Why, though, Tray? Why us?"

"I can't answer that, Troy. But I do know that a lot of people will have hell to pay. C'mon, let's get out of here."

"Sir, you can't leave. This is a murder scene," the officer said.

"We were having a fuckin' family gathering when these people dropped in on our party uninvited. That's all I have to say. Am I under arrest?" Tray asked, eyes full of fury.

"No, sir. But I can't let you leave until my supervisor says that it's okay."

"And who's your superior?"

"FBI Agent John Cage, sir."

"So where is he now?"

"On his way as we speak, sir."

"Well, he can meet us at the hospital. We're injured. Or do we wait for your boss while we bleed to death?" Troy asked.

"No, sir. I'll let him know when he arrives."

Troy, Jaafar, Tray, and Salvator walked out of the house and jumped into the Hummer. They exited the gates and looked back at what was left of James's mansion.

"Anybody need a doctor?" Tray asked.

Nobody answered. Everybody was in deep thought, replaying the scene.

During the drive to their destination, Tray pressed a button on his cell phone.

Ring, ring, ring . . .

"Hello?"

"Hey, Doc. This Tray. Meet me at the club immediately!"

"Tray, you know what time of the morning it is?" Doctor Hanson asked.

"Look, muthafucka, you worried about what time it is? Have you forgotten why you still have a fuckin' practice? You know what? You have a week to get my money and pack yo' shit up, then get the fuck out of this state."

Click.

He dialed another number immediately.

Ring, ring, ring . . .

"Hello?"

"Hey, sweetie. It's Tray."

"What's wrong, Tray?" Alesha asked.

"I need a nurse to look at a few friends of mine at the club."

"How bad are they hurt?"

"Not that bad. Cuts and bruises. Just bring your medical bag, baby."

"I'm on my way, Tray."

He ended the call.

"Jaafar!"

"Yeah, Tray. What's up?"

"Doc has to go to sleep immediately."

"I'm on that. I won't miss him," Jaafar promised.

"Did y'all get a make on them assassins?" Tray asked.

"Yeah. They're Saudis," Salvator offered.

"Sounds like the oil princes are mad about something," Jaafar stated.

"We talked about this before James left to do *The Oprah Show*," Troy said.

Tray made a third and final call.

Ring, ring . . .

"Hello?" a gruff voice answered.

"Hey, Chief. This Tray. Sorry to wake you."

"Oh no, Tray, don't worry about that. What's wrong?"

"We got hit in Slidell at James's mansion by a team of assassins. My bodyguards can't protect them in the hospital. I need you to send some men to the hospital."

"Who got injured?"

"James, Deon, and Luqman."

"Holy shit! I'll send some guys over there right now, Tray," the chief stated.

"Thanks, Chief," Tray said as he whacked the window

with his fist. "That'll buy us the time we need to find out which one of those punk muthafuckas sent the hit."

"I think I can narrow that down a bit," Troy anxiously stated, then dialed a number on his car phone.

"Hello?"

"Irvin, this is Troy."

"What's wrong?"

"Long story. But we got hit. James, Deon, and Luqman are in the hospital."

"What condition?" Irvin asked.

"Don't know. We slipped out to try to put this puzzle together. We'll check on them later."

"What do you need?" Irvin asked.

"The assassins were from Saudi Arabia."

"The oil princes?" Irvin stated.

"Exactly. Check to see if there was any movements or meetings between them through your sources and get back with us immediately."

"I'll call you as soon as I hear something," Irvin assured him.

"No. I'll call you within the hour. My phone was lost." *Click.*

"How many men you suppose you'll need?" Troy asked Jaafar as they merged onto the interstate en route to Club Ballers.

"Depends. Saudi Arabia is an altogether different type of fight. There's going to be hot, sandy conditions, and rough, mountain terrain," Jaafar said.

"We have just what we need then," Troy stated.

"What's that?"

"James visited Osama and recruited Taliban fighters."

"He *what?*" Tray inquired.

"Yeah. He brought back a hundred Taliban fighters to fight this war already," Troy stated.

"He's right," Salvator agreed. "I was with him. It's true. They would know that territory better than anyone we could find."

"That damn man is too smart for his own good. How could he have prepared for this?" Tray asked.

"He once said to me, it is best to be prepared for battle than to find yourself in a battle and not be prepared," Salvator expressed.

"Well, no sense in not using the tools at our disposal. I'll call Mahmoud at the compound and get them ready for travel," Troy stated.

Minutes later, they pulled into Club Baller's deserted parking lot. Tray was inserting his key when he thought about Dip. He forgot to call him and put him up on things, especially Deon. Dip had been chasing Kane's scent since the other day. Tray called Dip and alerted him about the attack on the mansion. Told him who was hurt and that they were all at Slidell General. He knew the federal cops would be crawling all over the hospital in search of answers.

Chapter 6

"I need two pints of blood, stat," the nurse yelled to the blood bank orderly. "Type O positive." The doctors had James on the operating table with four gunshot wounds.

"Get those clothes off and prepare him for surgery! Stat! Where was he hit?" Doctor Veja said.

"Two times, upper right chest, once in the right shoulder, and once in the leg," the paramedic stated.

"Where's that blood! We're losing him! I need that blood, stat!"

The heart-rate machine beeped, *beep, beep, beep, beep, beep*; then the lines started flattening. "I need that blood!" Doctor Veja yelled.

The nurse came with the blood just as the doctor was about to yell again.

"What the fuck do you mean, you allowed four people to walk away from a fuckin' massacre?" John asked.

"Sir, they claimed they were hurt and needed to go to the hospital," Officer Patterson replied.

"Did you ever hear of an ambulance?"

Officer Patterson just shrugged his shoulders, not knowing what to say. John looked around the house, then kicked another hole in the wall of the battered mansion.

"Where did you get your training at, Wal-Mart?" he asked the officer. The officer said nothing.

John wandered into the weapons room behind the bookshelf. *Damn, they certainly have an abundance of weapons to be lawyers,* he thought. "What type of lawyer needs an arsenal?" This only confirmed what he had been feeling. This family was connected to criminal activities in a major way, and he would not rest until they were behind bars.

"Officer Patterson, have you identified those bodies out in the yard?"

"No, sir. We did get a fingerprint analysis and bagged them to be analyzed once we return to headquarters."

"From their appearance, what nationality do you think they are?" he asked.

"They look like Saudis, sir."

"Very good observation. Get those identifications to me ASAP," John stated. "I'll be at Slidell General."

John had finally got a lead on his case against James and his organization. Now it was time to do some serious digging, while their organization was vulnerable. With James in serious condition, it would only be a matter of time before everything came apart. *Organizations always fall after the head collapses,* he thought.

"Malik, you can't make a trip down there at this time," Irvin informed him.

"Look, Irvin, that's my best friend we're talking about," Malik insisted.

"You can't get near this thing, Malik. It's political suicide!"

"I don't give a *damn* about politics when my friend is lying in some hospital near death. I should be there, regardless of what position I hold."

"James would've give a damn about this office if you don't. It's his and your life's work, damn it! He would never forgive you for making a selfish decision that neglects everything you've been planning. It's bigger than us, can't you see?" Irvin asked. "It's probably why he's fighting for his life now. In fact, it is why he's in this position. In James's mind, the cause will always be greater than any one man, even himself. He would be the first to tell you that," Irvin concluded.

Malik took a seat behind his desk in the Oval Office. He placed his head on the desk, then began speaking. "You're making all the sense in the world, Irvin. But so much is riding on James. I don't know if I can do it without him. Have you found out anything on the people responsible for this?"

"As a matter of fact, I know *exactly* who put this plan in motion."

"Who are these people, Irvin?"

"King Shalik Khalid, Prince Abdullah Ahmed, Prince Zamir ZanZia, and Prince Ahrah Ohani. They met at King Khalid's palace, then the next day, all three princes traveled to separate parts of the world."

"Where did they go?" Malik inquired.

"Colombia, Cuba, and Mexico. My best guess is that

they are trying to convince the drug lords to deal with them instead of James."

"Are they still in those countries?" Malik asked.

"As of this morning, they're still there!"

"Look, I want a team in all three places within a reasonable time to unleash all hell on them right now!" Malik commanded.

"Are we to take out the drug lords as well?"

"Are they cooperating with the Saudis?"

"I don't know that, Malik."

"Let's find out then."

"Who are you calling?"

"The presidents over there. I know they won't cooperate," Malik assured Irvin.

"Hello?"

"President Juarez, this is President Quinn."

"Hello, President Quinn. How are you?"

"Not too good, Miquel."

"How can I help you, then?"

"There is someone, a Prince Abdullah who has landed in your country with the intentions of depriving your country of the opportunities you and James agreed upon earlier. At this moment, he is supposedly meeting with Pablo Hernandez, trying to persuade him to go back on his deal with James. If he succeeds, your country suffers the loss."

"What do you need me to do for you, Malik?"

"I can put a team together within the hour and make sure the prince never makes it back home," Malik replied.

"If that is your wish, Malik. But is it that serious?"

"I've never mentioned this, but they sent a hit squad to James's home. James is fighting for his life, along with his sister and friend," Malik informed him.

"In that case, send your men. I'll make sure he doesn't leave my country," President Juarez assured him.

Malik called, then spoke with the other two presidents, and they also agreed not to let the princes leave their countries. All three presidents assured Malik that the drug lords would never give up their offers. James's deal was too good to pass up.

Finally, Malik called Troy to get an update.

"Hello?" Troy answered.

"Troy, this is Malik."

"Irvin must've got my message, huh?"

"Yeah, we've got that information. Look, three of the four people in on this are being dealt with. The fourth is in Saudi Arabia."

"Who is he?"

"King Shalik Khalid. I can handle this if you want me to," Malik replied.

"Too late, Malik. We have a team that already left for Saudi Arabia. We knew the hit came from there. We just needed names and coordinates."

"So your team is up on everything needed that will ensure they get in and out without leaving a trail back to us?" Malik asked on a secure line in the Oval Office.

"Our very best has gone on this mission. Mistakes don't happen with these guys. We have the now retired General McCloud heading the group, and you know about his work. The wars he has fought for the United

States is in the history books. We also have our top two assassins who are legends in their own right. Jaafar Ali and Salvator Dovinchi. Last, but not least, five of Osama's Taliban fighters have also made the trip," Troy confidently stated.

"Certainly looks like you've covered all the bases. I still may take an unofficial trip down there if James doesn't come around in a day or two," Malik informed him.

"Suit yourself, Malik. I know how close the two of you are, and I guess your presence is always a good thing. But what would James say to you bringing all that publicity to the situation?"

"You sound like Irvin now. But I see your point with my position as the president. But not as a friend. You must understand that aspect of me not being there for him," Malik expressed. "How are the other two doing?"

"Deon and Luqman are out of the woods. Another thing, there's an FBI agent by the name of John Cage down here getting to be a thorn in my side. Does he have a boss up there, or should I show him who's boss down here?"

"Actually, I've spoken to Irvin about him, and he's been asking questions about the wrong people. However, he's been put on a short leash. Just think of him as a little competition that keeps you sharp and on your toes. If you know someone's watching, the smarter you become because of it," Malik stated.

"You sound like James, now. Let me get this information to my team before they make it to their destination."

"Hey, Troy. That's the highest honor you can pay me, by comparing me to James. I don't really think we understand just how lucky we are to know him."

Malik hung up the phone, only to see his wife, Janice, standing there in tears as the news had gotten to her about James. Malik rushed over to her, and they embraced for the longest moment. No doubt, both were saying silent prayers.

Troy got General McCloud on the line ASAP.

"Hello?" he answered.

"Yeah, General, this is Troy. I have that information for you."

"That's good, son. You must've been reading my mind."

"Okay. Here are your coordinates: 367 east latitude, and 405 north longitude. You should find the palace there."

"Very well, son. Anything else we should know about?"

"I gave you what was given to me, General. I only wish now I was there with you and the team. But I let you talk me out of it," Troy said.

"Son, this isn't the place where you're needed. You're needed there. Your brother, I'm sure of it, was grooming you for a larger role, not this field work. You're the head now, son. And don't forget about the role you must play. If you die, the vision dies, and the dream dies too. As long as your brother is lying up in that hospital, every decision you make now must be in accordance with what James would have done. He knew the importance of those decisions no matter how big or small. This thing is bigger than your ego and vengeance."

"I understand that."

"Good! James knew what he possibly was getting himself into. But that didn't stop him. Death is going to come to you, son. Don't go through life sticking your neck out, thinking the guillotine won't swing your way. So make smart decisions with your life, because more than you depend on it, just as you depended on James. Anything else, son? I see our destination popping up over the mountains."

"No, General, but I needed that perspective. Sometimes we only think we're living for ourselves. But I know now it's bigger than anything I could've dreamed of. The best thing about it is that I get to be a part of it. Most of my life, I've had my brother there to shield me from hurt and pain. Now, I'm going to help shield him," Troy promised.

The army-issued Tomahawk helicopter with infrared night vision had landed an hour ago. It was hidden behind Mount Calibus, about a mile away from King Khalid's palace. The pilot listened for General McCloud to radio him for the pickup of the team with utmost importance. The general, Mahmoud, Salvator, Jaafar, and five other Taliban fighters were presently at King Khalid's palace. They had made it thirty minutes ago; that was the last transmission the pilot had received.

Mahmoud and the Taliban fighters had strategically placed explosives around the palace for exit purposes. Jaafar and Salvator had silently entered the palace, tossing a hook rope over the wall, then climbing it. They silently executed the king's men, one by one as they made their way through the palace. The night was calm as any other night unless there was a royal feast, but tonight wasn't the case.

Jaafar and Salvator, now working opposite sides of the palace, continued to sneak up on and kill the king's men as they neared the king's quarters. All that could be heard was the bullets hissing through the air as they left the high-power pistols and rifle barrels.

A couple more feet away was the room where they'd find the king. They had completely wiped out the top-level security crew. Jaafar turned the doorknob that led to the king's quarters. Salvator, seeing the door was locked, placed two pieces of small explosives at the hinges of the door, then detonated it twice.

Pop, pop was all that was heard.

The door dropped off its hinges. Jaafar caught it before it fell. He and Salvator again started moving, now through the dark corridors, peeking in and out of the rooms in search of the king. At the end of the corridor was a room with light illuminating from underneath. Movement could be seen. They were two feet away when King Khalid opened the door. Startled, he said, "Who are you men, and what do you want?" His face was full of concern.

"We came to bring you the same message you sent yesterday," Salvator menacingly stated.

"What message are you speaking of? I didn't send any message."

"Maybe the cries of the now-dead will refresh your memory." Salvator reached into his pocket, retrieving his phone. He then played the audio of Prince Abdullah being tortured in Colombia.

"Prince Abdullah, why are you here in Colombia?"

"I . . . I-I, ummm." *The torturer immediately slapped him across his face with what sounded like a steel pipe.*

"I-I-I-I," *the screams echoed in the room but went nowhere.*

"I'll ask you again, but in a different way," *the torturer stated.* *"Who sent you here, Pablo Hernandez?"*

"It was King Khalid."

"Who else is involved?"

"Prince Zamir and Prince Ahrah."

Click.

Salvator slid the phone back into his pocket.

"As I've said, King Khalid, you sent a message, and that message meant war. We accept your challenge," Salvator stated.

"More importantly is why we're here," Jaafar stated. "'Checkmate' is the word used when a king gets captured, right?"

King Khalid bowed his head as he accepted his fate. What else could he have done? General McCloud spoke through the earpieces to Jaafar and Salvator. "How long is this going to take, gentlemen?"

"We're on our way out now," Salvator stated.

Jaafar pumped King Khalid full of lead. The two men exited the king's quarters, running through the corridors, taking three steps at a time down the stairs. As they made their way back near the hook rope, one of the king's men appeared from the shadows. Jaafar was halfway down the rope as gunfire erupted.

"I-I . . . I'm hit," Salvator groaned. Jaafar was already on the ground. All chaos broke out as men poured out of the palace, but there was no turning back.

The Taliban fighters started detonating the explosives in and around the palace to slow the wave of men pouring out of the compound.

Salvator continued spraying round after round to keep the men from surrounding him. General McCloud spoke to Salvator through his earpiece.

"Where are you, Salvator?"

"I'm still at the wall. They have me cornered in, and I'm running out of bullets."

"We're under heavy fire down here. I've called the helicopter. Do you see any way we can rescue you?" General McCloud asked.

Salvator looked around, then at his leg that was busted up bad. He knew he couldn't make it to the hook rope without being shot in the back. His situation was a lost cause.

"No, General. Don't wait for me. The mission is complete."

Everyone heard the last transmission and felt bad about leaving Salvator, but he was right. They had to get to safety. The exchange of automatic gunfire continued as the team ran away from the palace. The Taliban fighters set off more explosives as the men exited the palace after them. All that could be heard were the screams after the detonations.

The Tomahawk helicopter appeared over Mount Calibus raining rockets on the men following the team. Within minutes, the pilot was able to set the helicopter down, and everybody made it back . . . except for Salvator.

Chapter 7

Dip sat in the corner of the hospital where Deon was recovering from surgery. He had dozed off, then woke up several times. He'd given the detectives all kinds of hell because they wouldn't allow him to stay with Deon. They were about to arrest him, but they called Chief Ryan, and he called Tray. Then he was allowed to stay.

Suddenly, Slidell General had become like a fortress. The police were crawling all over the place, trying to get information on the conditions of the victims. The media staked out, trying to get an exclusive on what occurred at the mansion of the man who was on the verge of hero status.

Dip strolled over to the bed where Deon lay. He wiped his eyes as a tear ran down his face. He thought about what she must've gone through as she lay peacefully in her sleep. Then he promised himself he would be there for her in the future. *Damn, I should've been there with her.* He wanted to be the first person she'd see when she awakened. Deon looked so innocent as she slept.

Suddenly, Joy walked through the door arguing with the security officer. "Man, why don't you just stand down and make yourself useful, like at a doughnut shop?"

"Ma'am, this room is off-limits to visitors," the huge Hulk Hogan look-alike stated with authority.

"It's all right," Deon stated as she remembered Joy from the party.

"Sorry, I have my orders, so you must leave," he demanded.

"Don't move. My girl said it was cool," Dip said, looking at the officer. He picked up the phone, then dialed Chief Ryan.

"Hello, Chief Ryan?" Dip asked.

"Speaking," he replied.

"Chief, it's Dip." He pressed the speakerphone button.

"Is everything okay?" Chief Ryan asked.

"Just a second, Chief." Dip pressed the mute button on the phone, then pushed it in the direction of the officer.

"Is everything okay, Officer?" Dip asked.

"I guess it is," the officer said, then hurried out the door.

Dip unmuted the phone. "Yes, Chief, everything is fine. We just wanted to thank you once again. Have a good night."

Deon was sitting up in the bed with her face twisted.

"Look at you, showboating," Joy said.

"Just helping a friend of a friend. And by the way, I'm Dip. Nice to meet you," he stated, extending his hand.

"Same here. I'm Joy," she said, accepting his handshake. Her dark chocolate skin, brown eyes, and shoulder-length black hair didn't go unnoticed. Dip thought that Joy was attractive and tall, at least five-nine.

Turning her attention to Deon, Joy strolled her 140-pound frame over to the bed in two fluid strides. And at thirty-one with her hair pulled back in a ponytail, she was as gorgeous as a young college freshman.

"How are you doing, Deon?" she asked.

"I've been better."

"I was on my way to sit with James, so I figured I'd stop in and say hello. I know we didn't get a chance to talk before all the drama."

"Well, Joy, my family does have their highs and lows, but we're only trying to make a living like every other family. We have haters, no doubt about that," she expressed. "Basically, we were warned by James that things were about to get dangerous once he revealed his discoveries. I think it's time we do some relocating and start living, thinking, and acting like extraordinary people. No matter how much we didn't want to change our lifestyle, we've been too accessible to the people who'll oppose what we're trying to accomplish." Deon grimaced.

"I agree," Joy stated. "I saw James's interview with Oprah, and as I thought about the change that will occur because of it, I figured there would be a tremendous backlash of opposition from powerful people all over the world."

"Girl, we definitely have to be smarter about everything."

"Right, so when do you think you'll be able to leave here?" Joy asked.

"Hopefully in a couple of days. Who knows what Troy involves himself in out there. I've been watching the news, and some very peculiar things have been happening in the world."

"He was with Tray the last time I spoke to Tray," Dip offered, to calm Deon.

"Still, Dip, you don't know Troy like I do. He hasn't

even called me, and that's a sure sign he's up to something," Deon said.

"You don't think he's supposed to be, considering the obvious?" Dip questioned.

"Actually, at the present time, hell no!" Deon responded. "This must be that testosterone elevation shit you men be on all the time. An eye for an eye is all it's about, huh?"

"Just like fair exchange ain't no robbery, either. What women seem not to understand is that you don't build empires by getting shitted on. You have to do some shitting, just like the hunter must hunt or be hunted. So it has nothing to do with testosterone levels, and everything to do with the laws of the land. When someone claps, you clap back—only harder."

"So how long does this clapping go on?" Deon asked, her thoughts twirling around in her head.

"Until only one man is standing, or the other is waving a white flag." Dip paced the floor, feeling dangerous.

"So what goes down when the flag goes up?"

"They still get dealt with one way or another. The law of the land says you never leave an enemy behind," Dip stated with conviction.

Deon threw her hands up in the air, then groaned from the pain. "You see, it never ends. And men just don't get it."

"Oh, we get it. But we get it right the *first* time, so there'll never be a second."

"Okay, I give up, Mr. Gladiator. Go right ahead and do you." Deon lay back and closed her eyes.

Joy wouldn't dare interject herself into that conversation. Deon was exhausted, so Joy waved good-bye to Dip, then slipped out the door.

Dip's need for action was turned up. He paced the floor for a couple of minutes, then came to a stop. He thought about something Keoka had shared with him. He started nodding his head. His face became meaner, angrier than earlier. He reached underneath his shirt and pulled out his nickel-plated .45 Desert Eagle handgun. He kissed it, stuck it back into his waistband, then exited the room.

The moment the door closed, Deon's eyes popped open.

Around the corner, James lay in bed after being in surgery for five hours. He was still in a coma caused by the explosion. The bar had landed on his head knocking him out instantly. The bullets were removed, but he was as close to death as one can be, then live to tell about it.

Joy Turner, the Tulane law professor, was there, constantly talking to James in hopes he'd hear her. She truly appreciated being in his company. She liked the way he would ask her a myriad of questions: who her parents were, where was she raised, what her profession was, if she had children, then patiently waiting for all the answers.

He also answered her one question: Where does James Johnson see himself in the next ten years? He took her to private places in his life and told her a story unimaginable to the average person. Yet, it left Joy thinking, without a doubt, that everything he visualized, present and future, was already in motion. That he wasn't just one-up on everyone else; he was light-years ahead of them. And he knew it but took no credit, because he associated all the present accomplishments it seemed with divinity. That he was only the vessel carrying the goods.

James had an unwavering belief that good will always defeat evil. Joy pondered while running her hand over his face pretending that it was their little thing with each other. Yet, the most beautiful thing he would ever say about himself was also the truest. James stated, "Of all the many things I desire in this world, the thing I desire most is to be good." Joy nodded her head approvingly, then gave him a gentle punch on the shoulder.

"Way to go," she had said and saluted him.

James had experienced a dramatic ordeal before he was stabilized. There were minor twitches and tics in his facial area . . . an occasional jerk of his shoulder and arm. But in the last few hours, those things had subsided. He was more peaceful now — no uncoordinated movements, other than his breathing.

"What are you thinking about, James?" Joy asked as she stroked his face, feeling the beginnings of a beard.

How intelligent she knew he was from their limited conversation. She now also knew she would do anything to have him. Today, she decided that nothing and no one would be allowed to come between them. Instantly, a sinister smile appeared across her face. "Chess," she said to herself as her phone vibrated on the bed. She looked at the caller's number, then sent it to voice mail.

"Nothing and no one," she whispered, then leaned in to kiss James's forehead.

"Sleep tight, my love. But you have to wake up, James. The world needs you. I need you," Joy whispered in his ear, then laid her head gently on his shoulder.

Tray and Troy were laid back at the club going over things. Alesha had patched Troy up; it was an in-and-out wound to his arm. She'd left several hours ago, en route to her job at the hospital. They had been looking at the news on every channel as the stations reported the incident in rotation. The fact of it being an assassination attempt made it a dire situation, Tray considered.

"This isn't good," Tray said with a look of concern. "Do you know of the agreements negotiated with the drug lords, Mafia, and presidents?" he asked Troy.

"Everything negotiated was put into a contract and is being held in our bank," Troy expressed.

"Our next move is to familiarize ourselves with those contracts, then reach out to them before they get leery of not getting what was promised to them. Trust me on this, Troy. If these men smell blood and think you're hurt, they'll try you. This must never happen if we're to succeed as planned."

"Basically, things are just getting started, so we're in the preliminary stages of the plan. Anybody who tries anything right now would put themselves in serious jeopardy. But we should send out reassurances to our future clients," Tray said. "We must stay ahead of the game if this project is what we know it is; it's too important to sleep on. We should expect that every move made against us will be a critical one. Every critical aspect of this new project must be secured. I've thought about an open end to this project that needs to be closed," Tray announced.

"The scientists," Tray stated bluntly. "James was the only person in contact with them. Remember that one of them has already gone public about his knowledge and role in the operation. Have all the patents and formulas been secured?"

"Knowing James, we have everything safely tucked away in our bank. This is way too important not to," Troy assured him.

"Well, our next move is to get over there to the bank and see just what we have or don't have," Tray stated. "Have you spoken with your sister yet?"

"No, I was going to get around to that today."

"I think we need to give her a call."

"We can drop by on our way back from the bank," Troy suggested.

"That's cool," Tray responded.

"Man, it really upsets me to see them that way," Troy confessed.

"I know, Troy, but just keep living, and you're going to witness a whole lot of what life throws at you. But the worst thing you can do is run away from it. How does it now feel to have the weight of the world on your shoulders?"

"It's different, Tray. I mean, in a spooky kind of way, man. I understand decisions have to be made, but I never experienced it to this magnitude. I just don't want to fail in making the wrong decision," Troy nervously stated, thinking about the incident with Kane.

"Your brother has been in this position all his life, my friend. Now you *really* understand what pressure is. Decisions are much easier when you make them with self in mind. But now, you're the strongest in the bunch; it's going to make or break you. From this experience, you'll know if you're cut out to lead or follow," Tray said, tapping Troy on the shoulder as he reached for the doorknob.

Chapter 8

Salvator was being held in a dungeon somewhere in Saudi Arabia. He had been tortured for five hours straight by the police. They demanded he tell them who sent him to kill King Khalid, but Salvator had no answer. The men at the palace had peeled off every fingernail on his right hand before turning him over to the police. The police torturers began where the others left off. They gave him electrical shocks until he passed out, then awakened him to repeat the process. Salvator had a nasty wound from the bullet he took at the palace. The conditions inside the dungeon were foul. The wound had become infected, and the pain was unbearable. Suddenly, the door opened, and a tray with some slop slid through. Salvator looked at the tray, then lay back on the bunk. He then thought about the homing device planted just under his skin. The general had suggested it in case anyone was captured. He smiled at the thought of the general and how good he was at preparing for war. His only wish now was that they make it here before his leg became gangrenous.

Just as he was thinking about the team, the door flung open. Two policemen strolled in, then each one grabbed his arm and escorted him through the dark corridors. Salvator's legs were dragging against the ground as the huge men kept turning corners and climbing stairs.

Suddenly, the men came to a door with plenty of lighting and a bed in the middle. The room had "infirmary" written on the glass. Salvator felt relieved that his wound would now receive some attention, as well as his fingers that were throbbing with pain. They opened the door, then tossed Salvator onto the bed.

A man in the corner was slipping on gloves. He wore a long, white doctor's jacket over blue scrub pants and shirt. He was definitely Saudi, and at the least, gave off the appearance of a doctor. He strolled over to Salvator, popping the gloves he had just slid on. The guards stood watch as the doctor began tending to him. He looked down at the blood-soaked pants and then back up at Salvator.

"You've been wounded pretty badly, mister. There's a pretty good chance you'll lose that leg. I am prepared to help you keep it, along with those fingers, if you tell us what we need to know, okay?"

Salvator just looked forward in silence, continuing to grimace in pain, his mind concentrating on when the cavalry would come.

"Very well. Guards, you can take him back to the dungeon," the doctor angrily stated.

The guards snatched Salvator off the bed, then dragged him back to the dungeon.

Back at the infirmary, the doctor called the head warden and reported that the prisoner had yet to reveal any information.

"Very well," the warden replied. "Maybe tomorrow he'll be feeling up to it. In a few days, he'll be facing the firing squad for his transgressions against King Khalid."

"That's *if* he makes it," the doctor said. "His wounds are very infected, and at any moment, he could black out and never come back."

"Well, that will be his fate," Warden Nikolic stated. "Either way, he will pay with his life."

"I take it the investigations into the three princes' disappearances are still mysterious?" Doctor Karlih asked.

"You have guessed correctly. However, now the counsel is short of four members of OPEC, and we think they acted on their own in approaching this American and his new discovery."

"I take it they didn't succeed, from the king's assassination and the three missing princes?"

"That's a correct assumption also, Doctor. No doubt, some big players conspired behind the scenes, but in the end, there will be a different outcome. Nevertheless, they have entered our territory, and we'll deal with our captive accordingly. In the meantime, our OPEC members support decreasing oil exports to make the American gas prices sky-rocket. We'll make them pay for even *entertaining* the thought of making us secondary!"

Mahmoud had just been dropped off in Afghanistan to merge with Osama the minute General McCloud detected movement by the homing device planted under Salvator's skin. Osama knew exactly where Salvator was being held, and he also knew he'd need most of his fighters to overtake the compound. They were a day's journey away from the compound, and there was no hesitation from Osama once he heard who was captured.

He and Salvator had been in countless battles together, both men placing their life in each other's hands. Osama knew how important Salvator was to James, also. Salvator was a man that was respected all over the world as well as feared. His friends that had been in combat with him called him "Whisper." Mainly because that's how his movements were; silent and deadly. Many men died, and the last thing they remembered was the whisper of the wind behind them. Those who were at war with them knew not to turn around. They knew Death would be standing there.

Osama smiled grimly as he marched through the deserts, valleys, and over mountains to rescue his friend. He was worried about how badly his friend was wounded. He knew the Saudis wouldn't treat him, and they would torture him for information at every turn.

They were making good time as they marched on. Their caravan of camels was packed with enough ammunition and rockets to start—and—end a war for a full day. The information he received was that the compound they were holding Salvator in was a prison, and at least fifty men staffed it. But, their real task was to take out the towers so they wouldn't be picked off. Then they'd planned on rocketing their way into the compound. Osama estimated arriving at the prison at 1:00 a.m. Perfect timing to catch them sleeping.

Troy and Tray were in the bank seated at a table inside the vault where the safe deposit boxes were stored. James had everything laid out as usual. The contracts for the factories, schools, the patents for the fuel, engines, and computer chips were there. The contracts for the Mafia, drug lords, and presidents were also present. *He thought of everything as usual.* Troy smiled at the thought.

"Everything looks to be in order," he said, leaning back, putting his hands behind his head.

"The money for the dons and the drug lords is to be drawn from these overseas accounts the portfolio here mentioned," Troy stated.

"A lot of money must be there because we have an estimated fifty-million dollars per month between the dons, and an estimate of seventy-five-million dollars per month between the drug lords." Tray opened the portfolio, then whistled. "Damn," was the only thing he could get out of his mouth.

"What's wrong?" Troy asked.

"It's not what's *wrong* that has my attention; it's how much money is in this account that's mind-boggling." He tossed Troy the portfolio. He opened it, slid his finger down the page toward the balance, and his eyes filled with amazement. The account had three point eight *billion* dollars in it.

Tray looked at the companies that James had invested in, which were Petroleum International, Wackenhut, Simco Corporations, J&J Gold Exchanges, and Pfizer

Pharmaceuticals. They were the cream of the crop companies James invested in. He had also invested in oil and gas, prisons, gun makers, and prescription drugs. James had millions of shares of each.

However, he had suddenly sold all his shares in oil, then transferred them to a computer company that would ultimately make the computer chips for the new vehicles. Next, he sold all his shares in prisons, then transferred those shares to En-Tech Designs, a company that would design the vehicles, then merge with La-Tech Machinery that would make the engines and batteries.

Nobody knew what was going on but James. He sold his shares at their highest, a day before the scientists were interviewed on CNN. The day after, oil prices dropped to their lowest in ten years. A day before he went on *The Oprah Show*, he sold his stock in prisons at their highest. Then, after the interview, the stock plummeted after hearing crime would be reduced and prisons closed.

But the biggest move of all occurred when James acquired the companies he'd transferred his shares into for an average of three dollars a share. Since the announcements, all the companies were averaging over a hundred dollars a share. The stock was still rising, as it had been updated by James the day of the assassination attempt.

Tray and Troy had concluded that everybody could be paid from this one account, starting in two months, as projected. There were also four other portfolios in the stack of papers.

"I'm scared to look at those," Troy stated.

"Well, your brother certainly was a busy man. We've

seen what we needed to at this time. Let's just make our next move," Tray suggested.

"You're right. Trying to keep up with James's movements will keep us here all day. We need to contact our friends and assure them that it's business as usual," Troy said with his best attempt at a poker face.

They stacked all the paperwork and portfolios back into the box, then strolled toward the door and pressed the button. A minute later, the bank manager slid the brass gate back.

"You gentlemen find everything you needed?"

"Yes, we did. And thanks for your help, Mr. Trazon," Troy replied.

"No problem, Mr. Johnson. And do know that my prayers are with you and your family." Troy nodded.

"Thanks, and you have a good day also."

They left the bank after being there for three hours. The Bentley was waiting for them as they exited the bank. Bodyguards were in front and behind the Bentley as the chauffeur opened the door. Tray spoke to the bodyguard in the Excursion in front through his two-way phone.

"Yeah, boss?"

"To the hospital in Slidell," Troy stated.

"No problem."

Troy picked up the cell phone, then dialed the number of Don Giodana.

"Hello."

"Don Giodana, how are you today?" Troy asked.

"Very good. But to whom am I speaking?"

"Troy Johnson, brother of James Johnson."

"Ohhh, okay. How is my friend doing, Mr. Troy?"

"He's resting," Troy replied. "Thanks for your concern. However, I'm calling to confirm that business will proceed as usual, and if it's not too much trouble, you can relay this message to your other friends."

"Certainly. As you wish, Mr. Johnson. No problem. However, my friends are telling me that your brother is in pretty bad shape, and they're a little worried."

"Unless one of those friends you speak of is God, I suggest you take my word for it. However, no matter what God decides to do with James's life, our contract still stands. But, as my brother has assured you, you don't have to accept this offer," Troy explained.

"I will certainly relay the message, Mr. Johnson. And do take care of yourself," Don Giodana said, then hung up.

Don Giodana wondered if their business deal would still be solid without James being in the fold. Troy didn't seem strong enough for him to place his investments in, Giodana thought. But what if James awakened to find that he had pulled out of his contract? *I guess we're going to have to see to it that he doesn't wake up,* Giodana pondered. He picked up his phone and began executing his next move.

The Excursions were pulling up to the hospital. It was noon, and as Troy and Tray exited the Bentley, the sun was beaming. The media was still outside hoping to get some news on the condition of James. One of the reporters from the local news rushed the Bentley as Tray got out.

"Mr. Johnson, can you tell us about the condition of your brother?"

"No comment," Troy stated.

They continued walking, now entering the hospital. Security was stationed everywhere. The two bodyguards walking with Tray and Troy set off the metal detectors that were just installed. Within seconds, they were detained by security officers. Irvin had sent the security team. They had strict orders to search and detain anyone suspicious or who set off the metal detectors.

The bodyguards were cleared, and they continued along with the rest of the crew en route to visit the fallen soldiers. The whole floor that James, Luqman, and Deon occupied had been cut off from all traffic. The doctors and nurses were handpicked.

Troy and Tray rode the elevator in silence as they thought about seeing their family in their most vulnerable state since knowing them.

Troy was thinking about the childhood times James, Deon, and he shared. He thought about their fights, and there were many, but the makeups were always the best. These were the times when that magic their mother often spoke about would always be present between siblings. He was feeling it now, as his eyes began to well up with tears. It was called true love.

Chapter 9

"I say fuck the world because the world has said fuck us all our lives!" Luqman expressed. "Look, we're in control now. Our gun is pointed at everyone else's head. So let's squeeze them triggers and make sure our clips are good and empty," he fumed.

"So, I seem to have heard something about some missing oil princes and a dead king over there in Saudi Arabia since you two went missing. What's good?" Luqman inquired with a smile. Tray and Troy stood silently and remained stoic, then looked at each other and grinned.

Convinced no information would be shared at the moment, Luqman continued. "Okay, there's no need for us to discuss anything at this time, but what we will need to do is not be so easy to find in the future. James spoke of this drama long before it happened, right?" Troy nodded his head indicating yes. "We're going to have to step our living arrangements up a whole lot better than what we have, gentlemen." Luqman retrieved bottled water from his nightstand. He took a sip and set it back down. "This empire is too big for all of us to be put at risk so easily."

"Damn, Luq. You seem to have a lot of shit on your chest. That's good, 'cause I know you're a true general at heart. That's the Luqman I need to see right now. Like it or not, from here on out, the game is being played for the kingdom. It's chess, just like James assured us," Troy stated.

"I second that," Tray intervened. "We definitely have to step our game up a few notches if we think we're big-league material. Man, them muthafuckas almost took all of us down in one sweep. That weak-ass shit can't happen like that ever again. Johnson Industries is worth billions, and we damn well supposed to be protected as such. Our new enemies are very powerful and will stop at nothing short of annihilating us, given the opportunity."

"So, what's our next step?" Troy asked.

"We prepare for war," Luqman replied. "That's all I've been thinking about while lying here with a bullet in my back! What we know for sure is we can't continue to be sitting ducks for target practice. We need more protection. And the only way we can do that and maintain our course is to split up. Then we can make our moves from various parts of the world. The countries that need us the most will protect us the best. That way, we're always in places we need to be, overseeing different projects. A moving target is always the hardest to hit."

"That just might work," Tray said. "What do you suggest we do with our present business?"

"We make changes," Luqman replied. "We can either sell them or hire people to manage them. In my opinion, with our present responsibilities to Johnson Industries, I hardly see a need to hold onto them . . . unless there's some sentimental value you're holding onto, that is. Think about it . . . We're going to be overseeing factories, schools, assembly plants, and board meetings that no doubt will produce problems that will demand we produce solutions. It makes little sense to travel back from different parts of the world to oversee clubs and corner stores."

"Makes sense to me," Troy interjected.

"Considering the information Luqman just offered, those businesses have become liabilities," Tray suggested.

"We have four major overseas positions we need to fill. Cuba, Colombia, Mexico, and Afghanistan. I didn't mention the United States, because once James awakens from the coma, he'll be better suited here and in Afghanistan, because of his ties to Osama. Each one of us can take one of the other countries."

"What about Deon?" Troy asked.

"I think she's better qualified to be the company's legal representative," Tray advised. "There's no doubt in my mind we'll need plenty of that. She can also oversee how we're perceived around the world, like our public relations firm too. The present firm will close to the public, then become headquarters for Johnson Industries."

"Has a tentative date been set for the production of the vehicles?" Luqman inquired.

"The contracts we read today indicate approximately three months from now, everything should be available for consumers," Troy said.

"Do you know of any reasons why we won't meet those production dates?" Luqman inquired.

"Besides what our enemies throw at us, we're good as far as the money to make this possible. We only need to get going on our individual duties overseeing things," Troy advised.

"Has anyone heard anything from the scientists?"

"No, and I don't expect to," Troy offered. "James kept them a secret from the world, and that's the key element keeping them alive this long. He was the only one outside of the scientists themselves that knew the research was going on. However, James left contact information in the bank's safe deposit box."

"All that's good, but we need them to begin teaching these technologies. The factories and schools have been under construction for quite some time, right?" Luqman asked.

"They'll be finished next month, from estimates of the construction contracts. We still have to set the criteria for students and definitely have to touch base with the scientists to begin launching our campaign," Troy assured them.

"Sounds like you have some calls to make — and fast," Luqman said.

"Sounds like you need to get well and out of this hospital," Troy joked.

"If I could've walked out of here, I would've a long time ago, and you know this, Troy. Another thing," Luqman began. "I've ordered a fleet of armored vehicles that we'll be chauffeured in from this day forward. I also have a meeting with a construction designer out of England who'll be dropping by. He'll be designing a fortress for James that'll feature state-of-the-art security monitoring.

"We have a hundred acres of land in Houma, not too far from the landing strip. That's where the fortress will be built. This will be James's waking-up present. There will not be another like it in the world. James will not have to leave this place for any reason. Everything will be at his fingertips. All his meetings will be held from within a video conference room via satellite from anywhere in the world. His staff will consist of butlers, maids, a tailor, a chef, security teams, computer programmers, etc. Nobody will enter the grounds not cleared through the sophisticated fingerprint analysis checkpoints that determine your identity in five seconds, tops. If an ant falls over the security wall, it will activate a silent alarm, causing a camera to zoom in on the exact location. Then, if a muthafucka is lucky enough to get over those twenty-foot walls, motion sensors will activate sweeping lasers that will shred them to pieces like a pack of ninjas," Luqman said. Troy and Tray stood in awe as Luqman spoke of the fortress.

"Do you think all that will be needed?" Troy reluctantly questioned.

Luqman just stared at him as if he'd asked a stupid question. Then a reassuring smile appeared across his dark, masculine face.

"Have you been down to room 413 yet?" Luqman curiously inquired.

Troy said nothing because his mind instantly replayed the scene where he and Tray entered James's room with all the machines beeping and pumping. James lay there helpless, still fighting for dear life, looking as peaceful as ever; but they knew that wasn't true. They knew he'd rather be here preparing for war, as they were now. But he was in another battle, a more vicious one with more drastic consequences, to be more exact. Live or die! Finally, Troy and Tray left the room that continued to beep and pump. Both men were in tears as they exited, not realizing they'd only been in the room for three minutes.

Sensing that both men had gotten his point, Luqman continued. "Everything we can think of that protects us from what happened to us will be needed.

"You see, in chess, the most important piece on the board is the king. Everything and everybody else protects the king, no matter what!"

Luqman knew Troy understood; drastic times called for drastic measures. Lives now depended on every move they made . . . or didn't make. You miss, you lose! This part of the game needed to be played with the option of taking a life, always on the table. Kill first, wonder about whether you made the right decision later. Deep within his thoughts, Luqman never even realized the two men had strolled out of the room. The only thing that mattered to him right now was war!

Troy and Tray walked down the hospital hallway, headed to Deon's room. They approached the door, knocked, then entered the room, finding her and Dip playing cards on the bed.

"Hey there, strangers," she excitedly stated.

"Hey, baby girl. How are they treating you around here?" Troy asked.

"I can't complain, other than you not coming sooner."

Troy just threw his arms up in the air. "You know boys will be boys. What's up, Dip?"

"It's gravy, playa. What's good?"

"Trying to make it do what it do, baby," Troy said with a smirk.

"I feel like shit. I'm just trying to make sense of this puzzle."

"What's the dilly, Tray?" Dip asked.

"Just looking in on the family. But I see you beat me to the draw."

"That's right, OG; you taught me well," Dip joked.

"I didn't teach you everything, so watch out, youngin'," Tray stated, then threw a few jabs at Dip to see if he could catch him slipping.

"I know you didn't. That's why I watch, listen, and pay good attention, even when you think I'm not," Dip explained, throwing some punches of his own that caught Tray in the side. "Getting rusty, old man!"

"Naah, just need you to feel as if you're gaining on me. But don't let that slow shit get you knocked the fuck out, thinking I didn't see those slow-ass jabs," Tray suggested.

The room burst out in laughter at Dip. Deon swallowed her mint and was choking on it until Troy patted her on the back.

"You got that, old man," Dip said, smiling.

"Oh, I know. But one day you'll get it too. I'm sure of it," Tray reminded him. The two men shared a hug, then Dip whispered in his ear, "What else are you dudes up to?"

"Nothing much. Going over plans about the company."

"Man, I wish I wasn't chasing Kane's ass all around the city half the night. Shit, I could've been there last night when them folks came through, shooting shit up," Dip said.

"Relax, my man," Tray stated. "One thing about chances. There's always another one coming around the corner. From the looks of it, you've found the right family to be a part of if you're looking for action. You'll definitely get your chance to play hero. We all will. Nevertheless, you may be saving your own life though."

Bring it on, Dip thought. *The only thing to fear is fear itself. Can't leave here breathing anyway.*

Tray continued. "More importantly is that you weren't there, because it kept you out of harm's way."

"Those men clearly had the element of surprise on their side—a deadly combination for us who didn't. I'm blessed to be here today, and wouldn't have wanted or needed you anywhere near that mansion, no matter how bad you wished you could've been," Deon genuinely offered.

"So, what's the latest?" Dip asked, quickly changing the subject.

Tray looked around uncomfortably. He didn't want to discuss any grimy business around Deon.

"Oh, we still working on a few leads, but nothing definite."

"Yeah, we know for sure this was a statement from any number of people James warned us about," Troy lied. "But, sis, we need you like a fish need water. Luqman has begun the implementation of some serious changes on how we're going to be doing business from here on out. I can't get into all of it right now, but it's needed—and urgently! When are you expected to be released?"

"In a day or two at the most, depending on how my wounds heal, the doctors said."

"Well, we have a few other stops to make when we leave, so give me a call if you need me," Troy said.

"Sure thing, big brother. Now, come on over here and give me some love with your sneaky self! Acting like I don't know what y'all up to," Deon replied.

"Just be careful," she whispered in Troy's ear.

"It's cool," he whispered back. "What you mean sneaky? *You* was always the sneaky one in the family. Might I remind you about Club Ballers? The night you snuck out and didn't invite me," Troy smirked.

"Boy, get away from me, Mr. Hot Boy of the Year! I get one date out of the year, and you want to be in on it. Pulleeese!"

"I just wanted to make sure you were in good hands, like a brother supposed to." Troy glanced in Dip's direction.

"Okay, Mr. Guardian. But who guards the guard?"

"Trust me, sis. James has that under control. Speaking of James, you don't know the half of what that man has going on in his skull. But that's another story. There's more pressing matters right now. Get well," Troy concluded.

Everybody embraced, then began exiting the room, headed to their vehicles. The bodyguards followed them closely as their heads moved from side to side in search of anything out of the ordinary.

❧✦☙

U.S. Attorney Roy Striker and FBI Agent John Cage met at Morton's Steakhouse inside Canal Place. John initiated the meeting in hopes of convincing Roy to open an investigation that would give him the go-ahead in using wiretapping against James.

"How's it going?" Roy asked, reaching out his hand and receiving a shake.

"Another day, another dime. You know the story."

"Oh yeah," Roy said, puzzled. "I thought another day for a cop was another couple steps toward breakup or divorce." The two men shared a laugh at the police joke, knowing it held much truth.

"What you got?" Roy inquired.

"Dying to fit pieces of this puzzle together. But I need your help."

"Sure, go ahead. What's the problem?" Roy said, nibbling on a hush puppy dipped in butter.

John took a deep breath for emphasis to make his theory look and feel more dramatic. "I think we have a pretty big problem that's growing bigger by the minute."

"You're speaking of James Johnson?" Roy inquired, still smacking on the hush puppies.

"That's right," John agreed. "I have four dead agents on my hand, and I'm only a month into this case. James Johnson and his organization are no longer a want. They're on my need list! He thinks he is above the law. That's got to change."

Roy sat a second, leaned back in his chair, and then

took a sip of water. "Okay, John. I'll extend my hand out for you as a favor. But I won't stick my neck out there on hunches. I'll open an investigation on what you have now, which ain't shit. But when he sends his big boys, I'd better have sufficient evidence to justify what you've done. If not, I'll shut you down faster than a KKK meeting at a Public Enemy concert," Roy assured him.

"I'm going to need wiretapping."

Roy whistled. "I can't authorize that. I still need my job, John. Bring me some concrete evidence or someone willing to talk. Shit, so far, our drug busts and stings haves netted us nothing on this organization. This operation is tighter than snail's pussy. We have to turn at least one of them from within the organization. What about the agent you planted?"

"One was killed at the assassination attempt in Slidell at the mansion," John replied.

"So, you have more planted?"

"Between just us, one of my agents remains in the heart of their organization. However, I have an agent hanging out whenever something is going on in the club they're always at. She's getting real familiar with the regulars but has not been able to hook up with our suspects yet. We're getting closer, though. We just need to be patient. I'm on my way back to James's mansion to see if I missed something. I never said anything about this, but there was a weapons room behind a bookshelf."

"No shit," Roy stated, surprised. "Why would a lawyer-slash-businessman need a weapons room?"

"That's another piece that doesn't fit in this puzzle.

The squeaky-clean image James is portraying has flaws. It's not adding up," John said with a curious smile.

"But as it stands, Mr. Johnson is backing out of the drug game, or might I say, the *illegal* drug game," Roy reminded John.

"One thing's for sure, He's one smart son of a bitch," John admiringly stated. "So, that window is closing fast if we hope to build a case against him."

"There's no time limitation on murder! If I get one iota of evidence, I'll prosecute him my damn self!" the U.S. Attorney promised. *If he thinks his Harvard education is going to help him once I get him on that witness stand, he's kidding himself,* he thought.

Chapter 10

Kane was laid-back at the new home he'd purchased in Atlanta. He was now awaiting a safe company. He'd purchased a six-foot, digital, stand-up safe, equipped with an alarm that notified the owner when it was being tampered with, by text message. He possessed over a hundred kilos of grade-A coke and a few million dollars. He was puffing on some Purple Haze reminiscing about the busy schedule he had this week. Now he had his own place furnished to his and Diamond's taste . . . and a master plan. They had traded the Chargers in for new vehicles. Diamond picked up a new Lexus 460 LS, with a candy-coated red paint job. Kane donned a Ford F-650, black, candy-coated paint job, fitted with chrome package everywhere chrome could go. He'd also placed much emphasis on security. Both vehicles were bullet-proof armor-plated, just like Dip's shit! He'd learned a valuable lesson that would keep him breathing longer.

As he was flipping through the channels, he stopped on CNN. The conversation the newscasters were engaged in was the attempt on James's life. He and Diamond had watched the entire Oprah Show of James's interview. He never met James, but he now understood where Troy had his brain fine-tuned. What a big brother to have. Kane looked at Diamond, then stated, "That nigga so smart it's scary! What if he really can do like he says he can?" Ever since that interview, Kane had thought about how to make the most of the coke he still had. More importantly, how could he capitalize off the street niggas' reluctance to take heed to what's being reported? Kane smiled, then took a big hit of the Purple Haze, now feeling like a true don. He knew niggas in the ATL didn't know anything about James to respect what was being reported. Besides, niggas from the street didn't watch CNN. They watched videos and *The Young and the Restless*, even when they got out of jail.

Kane now calculated himself to be two giant steps ahead of the streets, but there was nothing wrong with more. It was time for him to continue building. He had enough money to start buying all the coke on the streets of Atlanta. Then, once the drought comes, he would put major taxes on the coke he purchased without laying a finger on his grade-A coke sitting in his safe. He knew his coke could be cut three to one in a drought. So, for starters, he would have to buy out all the main suppliers, so that the streets couldn't get any. He flipped out his cell phone, placing a call to J-Rock.

"What's good, playboy? This Kane. I need to get at you whenever you can fit me in," he said once J-Rock answered.

"Just checking my traps. May take a minute. Look, let's get together in a couple of hours at C-Black spot on the Ave."

"That'll be perfect timing," Kane assured him.

This nigga claiming to be somebody in the ATL. I'm gonna see if he stuntin'. Maybe the nigga is half of what C-Black said he was, Kane thought, remembering Diamond's conversation from last night.

"Baby, have you ever thought about owning a business?" Diamond asked.

"I *do* have a business," Kane shot back. "I shovel snow!"

"Seriously, Kane. We can't live like Bonnie and Clyde. I want more out of this life for me. I've always wanted to own myself a business and be successful at it," Diamond admitted in a serious tone.

"What exactly would you want to get off into, baby?" Kane genuinely inquired. He knew Diamond was serious, so he had to respect her.

"I'd like to open a string of hair care product stores. I read in a Muslim newspaper that blacks spend three billion dollars a year on hair, but the Koreans own all the stores. To add insult to injury, they set up shop in our neighborhoods."

"That's some real shit, baby. But when did you start reading Muslim papers?"

"Oh . . . What? A sister can't get more conscious of her surroundings?"

"I didn't mean it in a negative way, but it's unusual that a sister would pick up that particular newspaper. However, I'm glad you did! I'm supporting you in anything you do, baby. If you feel success is coming to you in that form, let's do the research. I can't deny there's money in it; numbers don't lie. Shit, our only problem would be getting prices like the Koreans in order to compete. Our people's loyalty is to their dollar. Period. We need to be the cheapest to win," Kane concluded.

"You're right, baby. Them damn Koreans control the market. They drop plenty money when they order their products. Naturally, that's who the wholesalers want to do business with. They order truckloads of product. That's how they win. We been had the game all twisted by looking at it as being a hustle. We buy a little for a small profit. Hustling backward instead of working toward mass distribution, feel me?"

"I know exactly what you're saying, baby. In many ways, it's like the dope game, right?"

"Exactly," Diamond stated. "The name of the game is pay attention," she smirked.

"That's right, baby," Kane agreed.

"I can do this thing, Kane. All I really need is the resources to buy in bulk. This game isn't for hustlas. See, we've adapted the hustla's mentality; then apply it in the wrong markets. That's why we fail in so many business endeavors. But once I find out who they're ordering from, it's on and popping," Diamond promised.

"I know, love, and know that I'm behind you one hundred percent." Kane admired her independence.

A few minutes later, Diamond strolled out of the kitchen after preparing dinner. She heard a truck stop in front of the house, although Kane didn't. He'd fallen asleep with the remote in his hand. "Typical male," she said, softly kissing his lips.

"Wake up, sleepyhead. Them folks just pulled up."

"Damn, baby. I was just dreaming you wanted to open a string of hair stores," Kane said, stretching out his arms and legs as he got up from the sofa. "I swear that shit seem so real!"

"Boy, you tripping. We had that conversation before I went to the kitchen to cook. They must be throwing in a little extra shit in them drugs," Diamond insinuated.

Ding dong.

Kane strolled over to the door and peeped out. Two white boys were standing there smiling. Kane opened the door.

"Mr. Jones?" the skinny guy asked.

"You're in the right place. Y'all late too," Kane said. "How long will this take?"

"Oh, we'll be out of your way in about thirty minutes. We only need to bolt it down, plug it in, and then you can program in your security code. If you show me where it goes, I'll get right to it, sir," Wilbur stated.

Kane led the men to the master bedroom where the secret wall would be built later.

"My, my. This is a lovely home you've got here, sir. Yes, sir. One of the nicest on the block," Wilbur added.

Kane kept walking, knowing the man didn't like the fact of a young black man living in a nice home like this. He showed the men the area to place the safe, then left. "Holla if you need me," he yelled.

After smelling the aroma coming from the kitchen, Kane had gotten the munchies. He knew the pot roast wasn't ready, but he needed something to hold him until it was done. Diamond was pulling the corn bread out of the oven when Kane walked in and slapped her on the booty.

"Boy, you'd better go sit down somewhere before you starve."

"How long before that grub finish? It smells good."

"About thirty minutes. You want me to fix you a sandwich?"

"You already know. Shit, I'm starving like Marvin. Them boys down here. Purple Haze is torture, baby!"

"I bet it is," she agreed.

"What you think about James with this new fuel shit, baby?"

"Sounds like he's got his shit together, and it's been in motion a minute. Why you ask?"

"If it goes how he say it will, I'm sitting on a gold mine. I can wait and sell my product once the drought hit for whatever price and get no opposition," Kane stated.

"Sounds like a good idea." Diamond handed him the triple-decker roast beef and turkey sandwich. "What are you going to do once all the drugs dry up?" she asked, now pouring him a cold glass of Kool-Aid.

"I'm considering some business endeavors as you have. If this fuel thing is true, then I'm forced to get situated in another way. That may prove to be a good thing," he concluded. "Can't live like this all my life."

"It sounds pretty serious, the way them assassins came for him right after *The Oprah Show*. I wouldn't want to be in his shoes."

"You're right about that, baby. He dealing with big boys. When you're talking about stopping oil flow and drugs, it don't look good. That nigga put a bull's-eye on his back with his invention. Fuck 'em! I got to make this money, no matter what. They did me a favor by knocking this nigga off. I'd rather go up against Troy soft ass. Nigga always explaining shit instead of squeezing his trigger," Kane stated.

⚜

"Yo, Debbie. What's going on, baby?" Ray-Ray asked.

"Boy, I'm at work. What you trying to do? Get me fired?"

"Never that, baby. Look, I got a number I need you to check the incoming and outgoing numbers."

"Boy, hurry up and give me the numbers."

"504-906-1654," he stated.

Debbie's fingers went to work on the computer keyboard. The screen appeared.

"What number are you looking for?"

"I need to know the location of the calls, mainly the area codes."

"This number call log is full of Atlanta incoming and outgoing. This person most likely in Atlanta. Anything else?"

"Naah, that's what I was looking for. I owe you one," he promised.

"I'm going to hold you to it too," Debbie said.

Ray-Ray then dialed Troy to get a few things he would need.

"What's good, Ray-Ray?"

"Man, I have a location on Kane."

"Word? That's some good news. Shit, I got a thousand and one things going on right now. What you suggesting?"

"I'm putting together a crew to lay down in Atlanta a minute until he surfaces. How you want it handled once I get my hands on him?"

"First, he has something for us. Second, he stepped on Dip and Tray toes, so they want to see him before he takes his last breath."

"You know I don't have a problem with whatever way you want to do it. Ever since dude left, I been hot on his ass. Atlanta won't be big enough for the two of us," Ray-Ray stated. "How's the family doing?"

"Everybody out of the woods but James."

"Look, don't think I forgot about dude. I just work smart, so the target don't see it coming, feel me?"

"That's what I love about you, Ray-Ray. You laid-back, but you're very sufficient. Your friendship is as much an honor for me as mine to you. Let me know if there's anything you need for the mission, big or small. But when you meet up with Kane, give him a message for me," Troy said.

"That's no problem. What is it?"

"Tell him he couldn't run far enough or long enough to a place where I couldn't find him."

"Consider that a done deal, Troy. Look, I need some bait to catch a fish. What do this nigga love?"

"Drugs and broads! He'll run a country mile for any of the two," Troy said.

"Shit, I can recruit some broads when I get there. I'll need to get some drugs if you have any on hand."

"Man, I have a warehouse of that shit! Look, I'll have ten of them thangs waiting for you at the pawnshop where you pick up your artillery. I'll include some pocket change that'll last you a minute while you're hunting." Troy hung up the phone feeling satisfied, knowing Kane was almost in his clutches again. He thought of the motto he once shared with Kane. "*I want for my brother what I want for myself.*" He'd told Kane that and meant every word from the depths of his soul. "Now, all that's changed," Troy considered.

"Snap back," Tray stated. They were en route to the airport to pick up Tray's wife, Marlene. She had insisted that he not send a car to pick her up. Tray replayed their conversation before she left Italy to check on him.

"I'm okay, baby. You don't have to come all the way back here. Nothing is wrong with me. I'm good," he protested.

"Okay, baby. Just meet me at the airport once I call. And I repeat, *don't* send someone to get me, okay?" Those were her last words before she hung up the phone.

"What's on your mind, old man?" Troy asked, concerned about Tray having to be thrusted into all this drama now affecting his marriage.

"I shouldn't be picking Marlene up at a time like this, Troy. There's just too much going on. But women are so hardheaded at times."

"You do have a point, but do you blame them for loving us and our hard heads?" Troy debated. "We have to share some of that blame, you think?"

Tray shrugged. "It's crazy, man, because it must be their blame when they use love to justify becoming disobedient. They don't see the dangers as we do. They become blinded by that love, ultimately putting lives at risk as a result; bullets don't have names on them. What if she got killed? Will her love for me be the blame, or me for allowing her to disobey my wishes?"

"That's a hard one," Troy admitted. "Have you thought about retirement?"

"Since me, you, James, and Deon had our meeting, I did a few times, but none after the attempt on our lives. I've always dreamed of a day when my commitment to you all ended in success, and I really thought it was final. I guess that wasn't how it was supposed to have ended. So, now, I'm searching for another ending, a better one. That'll allow me to retire peacefully and gracefully," Tray considered.

"Well, now that the drug game is out of the question, what do your protégés do?" Troy inquired.

"I've been thinking about that too. Julio is due back from a trip any day now. Dip most likely will get in on what we're putting together at Johnson Industries. Trim will probably continue doing his own thing, pumping that dope. It's in his bloodline."

"So, Julio and Trim aren't smart enough to secure positions in Johnson Industries?"

"There's more to it than that, Troy. It's a matter of their lifestyles being the only reason why they're attracted to the game. As it stands, Julio and Trim are in a position of need by everyone they're supplying. They are winning right now. How do you tell the person who's winning the race to slow down or stop winning? Had they been on their game, they would've come to me a long time ago, once they acquired their wealth."

"I know what you mean. That game can suck you in, turn you out, up, and around if you're not smart enough to realize it," Troy shot back.

"Some think they're at the pinnacle of their careers when they're known by most in the drug game. That's the premature thinking of a fool with not much time left in the game. The true measure of their success in the game can only be determined by what they leave the game with. Then, on top of that, there are many regrets, not to mention lives lost. Success comes with a cost, and most times, I wish I could do it over. But in life, there's no do-overs. At one point, me and your father thought the game would be our only way out of the poverty-stricken ghettos. We had half of it right, but we never anticipated the price that would have to be paid."

Troy looked over at Tray, who was wiping away streams of tears that dripped down his cheeks. *What can I say to make him understand I feel his pain?* Troy pondered. *Probably nothing.* The truth being, he could not feel what Tray had witnessed — too many wars, too many deaths, with too many stupid reasons to justify the reasons why.

Tray pulled the bulletproofed Lexus 460 LS to the curb as they now observed Marlene waiting curbside. The bodyguards hurried out of their Excursions to retrieve her luggage. They quickly stood in front and on the side of Tray and Marlene as the two embraced. Then, they were escorted to the Excursions. Troy pulled off in the Lexus, along with a team of bodyguards in two other Excursions. He threw up the peace sign to Tray as they passed in separate directions. Then Tray flipped out his cell phone.

"Hello," a feminine voice answered.

"Maria, this Troy. I'm on your end of town and need to holla at you."

"No problem, Troy. I'll be here," she replied.

Troy hung up, then remembered how sexy Maria looked whenever he dropped in on Deon at her mansion. If James had not put him up on her, he would've made a play on her fine ass. How could a woman that fine be so dangerous? "Her beauty," James had assured him. "Men seem to melt in the presence of it." James also shared with Troy, some of Maria's many missions. If James hadn't been his brother, he'd call him a liar. This woman was a cold-blooded killer. Educated and paid her dues in the game. James met her when she was at her lowest; nursed her back to health, sent her back to school, then allowed her to take revenge on the men who left her for dead after killing her family. Her father was an underboss to the Scavino crime family but had been double-crossed by his hit man during a long-standing war with the Gugliodana crime family over territory. His hit man, Vito Santana, had risen in the ranks alongside Maria's father, Felipe Gortana. But on the eve of her seventeenth birthday, she couldn't have mistaken the man running away from her home after shots rang out. The man had been to their home too many times before that tragic night. It was definitely Vito Santana.

Maria and her high school boyfriend were parked several houses down as the unusual scene unfolded. She quickly gathered herself, then expressed to her boyfriend the identity of the man sprinting away from their home. The two teenagers slowly crept into the home through the door that had been left open. They searched the quiet home with a reluctance of what they may find. Then . . . There it was—the smell of fresh blood. They reached her parents' room, finding both with gunshot wounds to their heads that oozed blood and brain matter; eyes wide open. Maria hesitantly traveled the long hallway toward her brother's room, finding him also with a single shot to the head. Her boyfriend, Milano Santos, convinced her to hide out at his family home, then confided what they knew to his father. What they did not know was Milano's father was connected to the Gugliodana Family.

Maria couldn't sleep, as she had tried that night and was encouraged to do so, by Milano's father. As she lay awake, men suddenly entered the room she occupied. The men took her as she kicked, screamed, and cursed, protesting.

Oddly, she'd seen Milano's father standing there as she resisted. She wondered why he wasn't saying anything to the men, but planted across his face was an evil grin that told the entire story. Her family had been betrayed!

The men drove her out to the ports, then pumped five shots into her fragile body and left her for dead. Just so happened, James had gotten a crew together to unload some incoming cargo off one of their ships that night. As he exited his vehicle, hopped upon the pier walking toward the ship, he noticed the young girl's body. Not knowing whether to leave or assist, he jumped down, then checked for a pulse. There was one, but barely. He looked around, knowing what he should do. So he called his good friend, Doctor Jamison, for help. Charity Hospital would've wanted too much information, he decided. He got Doc to meet him at his private practice, along with his top nurse, which was Doc's wife, Mrs. Gloria. James relayed to the crew to proceed with unloading the cargo. He'd meet them later at the spot.

Maria recovered gradually. Then James listened to her story. He insisted that she enroll in college under a new name he'd produced and that she begin a new life. Then, when the timing was right, they'd get revenge.

Troy pulled up into the Riverwalk garage, then strolled into the mall. They owned five stores inside the mall, plus the bookstore where he was meeting Maria. For security purposes, he always left a bodyguard at the entrance of the store, in case he was being followed. He then went to the back of the store, activated the secret passageway, and entered the next store's office.

Maria was seated in the office as Troy entered.

"Hey there, lovely," Troy stated. *Damn, she looks good,* he thought.

"Hey yourself, stranger. How can I help you?"

Troy studied her for a moment, wondering if he should make his play. He decided to play it cool for a minute.

"Basically, I need a round number of how much product we have in the warehouse. Plus, I need ten kilos of coke sent to the pawn shop."

"No problem," Maria stated, as she began tapping into the computer that held a count of everything entering or exiting the warehouse.

The underground tunnels were built along with the warehouse as soon as James took over the ports. James agreed to first stake his money into the project, as well as the World's Fair held in New Orleans. He owned all the stores with the secret entrances to the port tunnels. The shipments of cocaine and heroin flowed like blood at a blood bank. The operation was flawless and had always been that way, just as James had planned it.

"There are 2,648 kilos of coke, with none on the way. Plus, 2,416 kilos of heroin, with none on the way," Maria reported.

"Sounds about right. Have you thought about where you want to work once we open the overseas factories?" he asked.

Maria shrugged. "Not really. Where are you going to be?"

"Not sure. Does it make a difference in your decision?"

"Certainly," she said, looking uncomfortable.

"Why is that?" Troy asked, curious.

Maria paused before answering. "Because you've always mattered to me, Troy. I see how you look at me. But you never say anything. I feel if I did, it would create a conflict of interest. Shit, did I *really* just say that?"

Troy smiled. He then gently grabbed her hands and stared into her eyes sincerely. He reached around her neck with his left hand and then planted a long, deep kiss on her lips. Maria began trembling as they kissed.

"Do you know how long I've wanted to do that?" he asked.

"Not as long as I've wanted you to!"

"So, where do we go from here?"

"Where do you *want* to go, Troy?"

"I think we can just explore each other further, with the possibility of us becoming whatever we create within our time together. No strings attached. I've wanted you a very long time and always had respect for the way you've carried yourself. Might have even been a little scared of you," he admitted. "Especially with all those bodies under your belt!"

"You've been listening to James too much," Maria replied. "However, I never gave someone something they didn't have coming to them. More importantly, I wouldn't be willing to give myself to you if I didn't think you were deserving. My only request is that you treat me as you would want to be treated. You'll get the very best of me, and I want to get your very best—or leave me be!"

"That sounds threatening."

"No, Troy. That's only a request." She smiled. "Besides, it would be foolish to threaten the boss."

"Correction. *James* is the boss; I'm only the brother."

"Same difference. But I think you've wasted enough time here. You know where to find me," Maria happily said, then planted a kiss on Troy's forehead. She then activated the trapdoor for Troy to leave.

Chapter 11

"Keoka, you ain't got nothing for pregnant bitches in here?" Tara loudly asked.

"Girl, you know this boutique is for fine hoes that don't mind popping they ass in the club 24/7. Not no pregnant bitches with fat ankles and an attitude to match. Besides, Kane gon' kill you if he catch that ass in a club carrying his child," Keoka stated. Diamond's cousin, Carla, was in the boutique, and Keoka knew this.

"Trust me, Keoka. That nigga won't lay a hand on me. Never have and never will. All the years we been kickin' it, that thought never crossed my big teddy bear mind. Shit, I can't wait 'til my graduation to be with his ass again."

The girls in the shop were ear-hustling something serious. This was top-of-the-line gossip going down. Straight off the press, the ink still wet!

Tara began bragging about her travels with Kane to Daytona Beach for Spring Break and shopping sprees at the Galleria in Houston. She pulled out her wallet to show off the pictures, in case no one believed her story. Every second Tara continued talking, Diamond's cousin, Carla, kept inching closer.

Keoka, being the instigator, poured a little gas on the fire, "Girl, when is the baby due?"

"Kane Junior is due February next year. And I can't wait!"

Carla stepped from behind a clothing rack with fire in her eyes. "Bitch, you around here on Kane's nuts like hair, as if you matter. As I see it, you can't be all that important if you're here, and he's somewhere else, with a face full of somebody else's pussy!"

"Who are you, stupid ho?" Tara asked.

Carla chuckled. "That's not important! But since we been here, you've been on this nigga's jock like you're something more than a jumpoff! Ain't you one of them hoes he left behind?" Carla shifted her weight to one leg, smacking on some gum, awaiting an answer.

"For your information, ho, he left me exactly what I needed. Money! Who gives a lovely fuck about who he took with him? So what! Let that ho take the chances," Tara shot back with a smile. "Oh yeah, in case you don't know who I am, and you don't, let me introduce myself! I'm that smart bitch in his crew of bitches. Now *you* figure it out." Tara slapped her platinum credit card on the counter for Keoka to swipe.

This bitch going hard as a muthafucka, Keoka thought as she swiped the credit card, peeping at Carla about to lose her cool.

"Furthermore, if you wouldn't have been ear-hustling, your feelings wouldn't have gotten hurt. That should teach you something."

"Bitch, you in here mouthing off like you 'bout that. Don't let yo' mouth overload your ass," Carla suggested.

"Look, hater, or whatever your name is. Your uncomfortable ass found me here, first of all."

Carla had closed in on Tara like a cheetah, then

slapped her face so hard, it left a hand print. Tara never got another word out. Like a young Mike Tyson, Carla was in Tara's space. The two of them were now tearing it down, scrapping like they were in Las Vegas at the MGM Grand Hotel. Tara managed to grab hold of Carla's hair, after taking two quick slaps and a duck that caught her on the temple and almost took her out of the game. But to everyone's surprise, Tara was suddenly the one on top. She was connecting with pin-point accuracy, and it was some hard shit! She then threw an uppercut as if she'd practiced it with Muhammed Ali. Carla's nose began to run like an inmate who'd just escaped. Blood was leaking everywhere as the once-predator had become the prey. The store was becoming a mess, so Keoka decided that the winner had been declared.

"Heyyyy . . . Y'all gots to break this shit up before my shit get damaged in here," Keoka yelled. Then she immediately came around the counter to get in between the women's mix. "One of y'all come grab one of these hoes," Keoka shot back at the customers. The women were still chicken-fighting before the big girl named Barbara stepped in.

"Now, none of you hoes swing," Big Barbara demanded. "Because if you hit me, I'ma deal witcha myself," she said, sounding like a fierce gladiator. After hearing that, it convinced both women to call it quits. But they were still mouthing off to save face.

Keoka handed Carla some napkins. "Now, go in my bathroom and clean yourself," she told her.

Carla went into the back as she was told, not knowing

what her face would look like. Keoka grabbed Tara's bag, slipped her receipt in it, and then told her she'd call her later.

"That's what's up," Tara confidently stated, "'cause these stupid hoes got me fucked up!" She snatched the bag off the counter, then twisted out the door, knowing she'd punished her opponent.

Minutes later, Carla strolled out of the back, looking like she had an allergic reaction.

"Girl, why don't you just chill. Y'all fought, and it was what it was. You got off on her first, so you should be satisfied with the results," Keoka expressed.

"Sounds like you're taking sides or something," Carla suggested. "We cool, Keoka, but you can get it too!"

Keoka's head spun around like the little white girl's in the movie, *The Exorcist*. She couldn't believe what she was hearing.

"Look, Carla. Your feelings may be hurt now, but make no mistakes about it. I am who you know I am! I might can understand this coming from somebody who don't know, but you know my work. So don't play yourself!" Keoka shot back, then walked up to Carla and pointed a finger in her face. "All the bitches I done beat down for yo' ass. Ho, pulleeeze!"

"You right, girl. My bad. That bitch got on my nerves with all that yapping," Carla confessed.

"Shit! She got on more than yo' nerves. Bitch, you gots to chalk that up as a loss!"

Carla gave her a little half-smile, then shook her head, agreeing. "Girl, you know when a lame get lucky, a player ain't got a chance. Look at how Busta Douglas beat

Mike Tyson. Shit, that bitch acted like she was fighting for dear life!" she responded. "But one thing's for sure," Carla contemplated. "Two mountains may never meet, but two people always will!"

"That shit sounds good, but do you really want to go there again? Because that shit didn't look like no luck."

"Don't worry, bitch. I'll make sure you get the news first. Once I do this ho something dirty, 'cause yo' ass acting like a fan and shit," Carla replied.

"Good luck. Some people don't learn. Sometimes they get what they're looking for. So, be careful what you're asking for. You just might get it," Keoka smiled.

"Where you at, Trim?" Dip asked.

"Just leaving the hospital. Why?"

"I just got a call from Tray, and I'm headed toward the club. Julio supposed to be over there also."

"What's going on?"

"Don't know. But I do know I have a missed call from Tray but didn't get the message until I got outside. I'm about five minutes away. You know how I get down in this Porsche," Dip stated.

"I'm pulling out now," Trim said. "Oh yeah. I received a call from Ray-Ray today. I think he couldn't get in touch with you, either. But dude seem to think your boy Kane is in Atlanta. He supposedly has gotten a team together and is about to roll out there."

"That's some very good news. Do they know his exact location?"

"Not to my understanding. But they figure to lay out there a minute until dude surfaces anyway. Shit, a nigga like dude can't hide. He loves the limelight too much."

"That's exactly right. You can't pay him to do the smart thing. Money goes to his head and . . . Word is, he took a lot of it from Troy," Dip stated, as he pulled up to the club with Young Jeezy pumping through the sound system in the Porsche.

About the same time, Doctor Hanson also pulled up, sporting a new Maserati. He was cautiously making his way toward the front entrance, holding a bag of money that he owed Tray. In his heart, he wanted mercy.

Everybody strolled into the club as the smell of cigar smoke filled the air. The club was dimly lit, just as the dancers and their customers liked it. The bodyguard took account of everyone entering, then immediately informed Tray, who was seated in his office, observing everything on the video equipment. His nostrils flared once he saw Doctor Hanson. He immediately called Jaafar and ordered him to come dispose of the doctor. He thought about how the chump questioned him when he really needed him.

Julio was seated at the video poker machine passing time as Tray, Dip, and Doc strolled over.

"What's good, Julio?" Dip said.

"Hey there, Dip. What's happening, Trim?" Julio inquired, giving both men a handshake and a hug. "Man, I'm just trying to maintain in this dirty game. Feel me?"

"Looks like you're doing a damn good job, judging from the new jewels you sportin'," Trim said.

"Damn," Dip remarked, "you had to have paid a

pretty penny for them diamonds, for real. Them mutha-fuckas look like blood diamonds!"

"Don't know all about that, my brother. But the game has been good to me," Julio admitted. "Shit, somebody has to make this game look easy. You don't mind if it's me, huh?" he asked, with arms extended, showing off the rest of his stylish attire.

"Get your shine on, 'cause back in the game, the motto was 'don't hate the playa, hate the game'," Trim offered.

"See, that's why you're my nigga, even if you don't get no bigger," Julio agreed.

"Yo, fellas. Tray said y'all c'mon up," Deebo, Tray's bodyguard said.

Everybody got up from their seats, then headed upstairs.

"Oh yeah. Not you, Doc. You can hang loose. But I'll take this off your hand." Deebo took the money bag from Doc, then pushed him back into the chair. "I'll be back for you in a second."

The three men strolled upstairs and into Tray's office.

"Have a seat, gentlemen," Tray stated. He continued to look over paperwork, then suddenly looked up.

"First of all, I think all of you are aware of this recent technology James has discovered, right?" Everyone nodded. "As you know, there are some major opportunities out there for people in our positions, in knowing James. I've known him all his life and was best friends with his father. Men, this opportunity is too big for me to pass up. It's basically a hustler's dream to come across this type of investment opportunity.

"However, what may be a good thing for me don't necessarily have to be the same for the next man. I'm not in a position to tell any of you what you should do with your money or your life. I've nurtured all of you to be your own man, and I think I've done a pretty good job of it. Hopefully, your leadership capabilities are what motivates you when faced with the tough decisions in life. I'm making one tonight, as I'm announcing my retirement from the game." Tray paused for emphasis.

"For all the wealth the game has given me and loyalty I've given it in return, I leave it not being owed a dime or owing the game nothing. More importantly is that I left it as I found it! I didn't add anything to it, nor did I take anything from it! It was perfect when it was passed down to me; then you all receive it in that condition. But if you decide to pass it on, as I have to you, remind whoever receives that knowledge that the game is worth more in its original condition than it'll ever be worth if you add or take away from it," Tray concluded.

He then tossed each man a key that belonged to a storage container.

"There are fifty kilos for each of you. I only want the money that's owed to me by your crews on the street. My books say that's an estimate of a little over three million apiece. I advise you to use your heads in future decisions with those drugs and your money. Nevertheless, if you're up on James's technology, then you know drugs will soon dry up. I know you're saying that's impossible, but I'm telling you as a friend: don't bet against him on this one! It was impossible in our minds because nobody ever tried it."

"Damn, man. You sounding all serious and shit. You sure you're not about to croak?" Julio asked.

"Shit! I never thought you'd give up the game," Trim admitted. Dip just lay back and played it cool, soaking up the game.

"I'm healthy, men. Just take my advice," Tray emphasized. "Tonight, I'm taking bids from you men for the sale of my club. There will be no more use for it. My time and money will now be invested in Johnson Industries."

Tray slid three pieces of paper across the desk to the men seated in front, and three pens. "I'll accept all reasonable offers, so don't insult me. I taught you better. So I'm owed better," Tray insisted.

Dip scribbled something on the paper, folded it, then slid it back to Tray. Trim took his time but finally came up with a number he could live with. Julio was last in sliding his offer to Tray.

Tray looked at the slips of paper, then smiled. "In all fairness to everyone, I'll show all the offers because we're family, and I'm a man of my word. No picks and chooses in this business." Tray slid Julio's bid to Dip; then Dip handed it to Trim. Next, Tray slid Trim's bid to Julio, who slid it to Dip.

"Trim had the winning bid, which was two million dollars," Tray announced.

Julio, who thought he'd bid the most before seeing Trim's bid, asked, "How much did Dip bid?"

Tray smiled as he knew Dip was the cream of the crop within his organization. He slid the slip to Julio; then Trim leaned over to look at the bid. Both men looked puzzled because all the paper contained was a smiley face and a zero scribble beside it.

"Explain to them why you didn't bid, Dip," Tray suggested.

"Did you not just explain that this latest project was a hustla's dream?" Dip stated. Tray nodded.

"Let's see. Hmm . . . If this project is a hustla's dream, then that must mean more money with fewer chances I'll see the penitentiary again. Also, the only way a man would sell a gold mine would be to purchase a diamond mine," Dip implied. Knowing Tray approved, he didn't want to rub it in. But once the drugs dried up, so would the big ballers' bank rolls. *Club Ballers is for ballers! When the game becomes extinct, who's going to buy them expensive bottles of Dom P at a couple hundred a pop? Or, even that hundred-dollar entrance fee? Oh yes, the name of the game is pay attention*, Dip thought, and kept grinning.

"Anyway, gentlemen, if there's any other business, you know how to reach me." Tray stood, then embraced everyone. They all went downstairs into the club and popped bottles of Dom P.

Ten minutes earlier, Jaafar had strolled into the club, catching Doc Hanson playing the video poker machine with his back turned. He stood behind Doc, then plunged a twelve-inch ice pick into the top of Doc's skull, causing only a small amount of blood to spray up into the air. Then, Doc's body immediately went limp.

Tray had watched the entire episode on the video monitors located in his office behind where Dip, Trim, and Julio were seated. Everything occurred without them knowing a thing. Doc's body was carefully chopped and hacked to pieces, then eventually fed to the fish in the Gulf of Mexico. *Never forget who buttered your bread, and never seem more important than your greatest ally,* Tray thought after the hit was completed.

Chapter 12

Osama and the Taliban fighters arrived at the prison a little before 1:00 a.m., as they had estimated. Three guard towers surrounded the prison in a triangle formation. Night vision goggles allowed the fighters to see into the towers. The snipers aimed at each guard inside the towers, then simultaneously squeezed off shots from the high-powered silenced rifles. Blood splattered throughout the tower windows, confirming the destruction that had been set forth. Osama then looked at the positioning of the implanted homing device inside Salvator. Once he had coordinates, they strategically moved in position closest to the signal.

On Osama's command, they launched rockets into the entrance gates. The fighters stormed the compound, blowing away the gates that led them inside the prison. They caught prison officials completely off guard, as weapons had to be issued to prison guards from a weapons room under lock and key. The night warden hurried in a frantic pace to issue the weapons after opening the room. He wondered what happened to the tower guards and their failure in alerting them.

Meanwhile, Osama and some of the fighters had made their way halfway through the prison. They were slaughtering unarmed guards without remorse, a testament to their status as deadly assassins. The men trotted through the dungeon corridors paying close attention to the signal as it got stronger. Guards within the dungeons had yet to receive weapons, only their standard-issued whistles, handcuffs, and billy clubs. That would also be the reasons for their deaths. All that could be heard throughout the dungeon walls were the screams of once-valiant men.

The warden managed to get weapons to his entire south wing; then the guards rummaged the prison in search of the intruders. They hurried around corners that led them to the dungeons where most of the screams were heard coming from.

But as they rounded the final corner, they were greeted by Mahmoud kneeling on one knee with a rocket launcher seated on his shoulder. The guards tried to turn back, but fate would not have it. It was their birthday! The missile left the tube with fire shooting from the back end. The first five who caught most of the blast would be closed caskets! There were no survivors to the destruction the rocket inflicted. The entrance to the dungeons from that end was now sealed off.

Other Taliban fighters were posted at other entrance points by Mahmoud as he scurried through the dungeons to catch up with his cousin, Osama. The fighters would not leave the points if their leader was inside; they'd die first.

Osama was still trotting through the dungeons with his AK-47 in hand. Then he heard a beep once he passed one of the rooms. One of the Taliban fighters ran over with the ring of keys taken from a deceased guard, then opened the door.

Osama sent up a silent prayer to Allah, hoping Salvator was still alive. Then, there he was. Salvator stood on his one good leg in the darkened corner of the room, not knowing what to do. Then Osama stepped through the door's entrance and stated, "As-salaamu alaikum!"

Salvator limped toward his friend; then the fighters immediately entered the room. Each took an arm, then proceeded to escort Salvator out of the dungeon. The corridors were clear as the fighters were staked out along the path that led them back to the exit of the prison.

The prison looked deserted, as the Taliban had spread throughout it as if they were cancer, killing everyone in their path. As they surfaced from out the dungeons, Osama and his men continued planting explosives. As much as Salvator hurt, he could not conceal the excitement of the rescue.

Minutes later, Osama, being the warrior he is, still was detonating explosives behind them and firing his AK-47 at the few guards that were firing from another part of the prison they had yet to reach.

As everyone hurriedly exited the front gates into the darkness of the hills, Osama turned to look at the little compound now a half mile away. He handed Salvator the detonator. Salvator accepted the detonator, then limped on his one good leg to the edge of the hill they now stood atop. He leaned on Osama to brace for the impact of the explosion. The next thing that occurred could only be compared to a Fourth of July celebration. The entire compound erupted in flames, illuminating the sky's vast darkness in the middle of the desert. The ground shook for miles around; then the two friends smiled, mounted themselves upon the camels, and rode off into the mountains.

Thousands of miles away, the Tomahawk helicopter was being serviced at a base at Camp Lejeune. General McCloud was seated behind his desk, still concerned about his friend, Salvator. He had just flown back after dropping off Jaafar and then the Taliban fighters that managed to survive the mission back at King Khalid's palace. The retired general now patiently waited for any word back from Osama to come pick up his friend, be it dead or alive. To him, Salvator would always be a war hero, no matter what! His friend had willingly stayed behind enemy lines countless times, but the general knew it only took one fatal set of circumstances to end the streak. Nonetheless, the old general decided he would not leave the camp until he heard of the warrior's fate.

J-Rock was seated in front of C-Black's new dancer, Ebony. He'd arrive at Ecstasy an hour early to get a first sample of the young tenderoni. He knew the other players were due to arrive at their usual times and would indeed hurt his game. He was grateful that C-Black let him in on all the new meat first, being he was VIP worthy and would spend major bread.

Ebony was truly a Grand Champion at what she did, and she did everything. There was no such thing as can't, ain't, or won't in her vocabulary. Her motto is always to let your wallet beat your dick out! But many days, Ebony had been gaffled by niggas claiming to be this and that to obtain her services. So after ending up with only a wet ass and a promise that she knew was no more reliable than a refrigerator would be in hell, she developed her motto! She switched her game up drastically, taking no prisoners nor accepting any credit. She'd become real popular on the strip scene, and then even managed to appear in a few flicks, but the unfortunate death of her friend, Lisa Lovely, who contracted AIDS from a top dick's man in the industry, forced her into retirement. Occasionally, she would accept an offer she couldn't refuse, but it was always protected sex.

Ebony met C-Black through one of her friends that stripped in another one of his clubs. C-Black's clubs were top-notch in Atlanta, and so were the many beautiful women who displayed their goods there.

So far, so good, she thought as J-Rock dropped another grand in her lap as she grinded, weaved, and popped her pussy in front of him. *And the night is still young*, she reasoned.

Suddenly, as she was twirling on the pole, a big nigga with dreads strolled over to her stage, dripping in diamonds. Dude was swagged out in Prada and Gucci. Kane stood to watch Ebony a second, then slid into the chair next to J-Rock, bobbing his head to Jay-Z's new joint, "Bam."

"What's good, my nigga?" J-Rock asked.

"Basically, my nigga, I'm trying to build my own

White House. But for me to achieve that goal, I need a lot of bricks," Kane said, looking for a response.

"It takes a lot of money to build a brick house, my man. You sure you don't want to start with a room?" he shot back.

Kane laughed at the remark. "First of all, J-Rock, money isn't an object for me if the price is right. So the only question before us is whether you have the connection to assist me. Then if so, we can talk numbers, quality, and quantity. I deal in mass distribution, so money comes back tenfold. I really don't have no time to waste, so you'll never catch me crumbing. I need hundreds of bricks if that's not out of your league. As you can see, I'ma big nigga."

"Okay, okay. I see what you're saying, homeboy. I can get at my people to assist you with your project. I must admit, your order is too big for me. Then, I'm not one to get into business not my own. But you seem like competition for me, you know what I mean?" J-Rock insinuated.

Kane leaned back, then slung the dreads out of his face as he now considered the words that would eliminate J-Rock's concerns. "I always was told that competition is a good thing," he began. "Second, sometimes we get too comfortable in positions . . . to the point we lose the hunger to keep on building." He glanced at Ebony a few seconds, then smiled.

"However, that's not my problem, nor focus in competing with anyone. I motivate myself — *that's* my competition! Always have strived to be the best, J-Rock. Never considered anyone above me to have to think about catching up, nor knocking the next man. No, my brotha. You're definitely not any competition of mine, and I say that with much respect to how you gettin' down. But if you can't supply me, how can you be my competition?"

J-Rock stayed seated, bobbing his head, eying Ebony with his poker face. "I think that's a very good point you make. So, that settles that," J-Rock said.

"Make no mistake; I'm not here for territories. I invest in drugs with drug money, and I'm sure we won't be dealing on the same level. Your spots are safe from my dealings. That's my word. I wouldn't be coming to you with my business if I had planned on stepping on your toes. But had it been, it would've been a perfect storm with no words spoken, feel me?" Kane inquired.

J-Rock smiled, very amused at Kane's honesty. "I feel that, big homie. Like a naked virgin and me in a Jacuzzi."

"Now, what I need for you to do is get on your job, so I can start building me a house. If the prices are right, you may be able to retire shortly after me," Kane bragged.

J-Rock studied Kane for a second, then took a sip of his Incredible Hulk. He liked Kane because the nigga had his own style, and he was the type of nigga that fit in anywhere. However, Rock had been schooled by the best too. And it was always told that everything shiny wasn't gold. He knew homework would have to be done — nothing personal, just business. *Many niggas lying in the penitentiaries wish they'd done some background checks before they placed themselves in harm's way.*

"I got you, big homie," J-Rock said. "I'ma do some

checking, then definitely give you the lowdown if it can go down!"

Kane then stood, tossed a few hundred on the stage, gave J-Rock a fist pound, and then headed for the door. He stepped into his F-650, then decided to give C-Black a call.

"C-Black speaking."

"Ol' stupid-ass nigga. That's how you answer yo' phone?"

"Nigga, fuck you! And stay yo' long-hair ass out of my clubs when I'm not around to watch yo' freaky ass!"

"Damn, nigga! What you have, a fuckin' Skycam in that muthafucka?"

"It's called technology. You better get up on it. Oh yeah, guess where I'm at, playa?"

"You sure you want me to guess that?" Kane asked.

"Stupid nigga dot com, what you think?" C-Black stated.

"Okay, okay. Let's see. Hmmm. I got a good guess."

"Would you like to share that guess?" C-Black said, getting impatient.

"At your gay lover's house, sucking his balls," Kane laughed.

"You's a bigheaded stupid nigga," C-Black shot back.

Kane was out his mind, laughing as he knew he'd gotten the best of his boy.

"No, nigga. Once I saw you enter my club, I headed over to your house to holla at Diamond's fine ass. You always say what's yours is mines, so like Frankie Beverly says, I want to thank you! Oh yeah, we just finished. You want to talk to her?"

"That shit not cool, C-Black. You been screaming Diamond's name since we left the penitentiary!"

"You right, and now she's screaming mines. Now, do you want to speak to her or what?"

There was only silence on the other end of the phone.

"She just finished brushing her tongue—I mean her teeth," C-Black threw at Kane. He knew from the silence, Kane was out of his element.

"Damn, nigga. You didn't tell me the girl could cook! Peep this, fool," C-Black began. "I just was served some tender pot roast, string beans, candy yams, and my favorite, just like Moms used to make. Some golden-brown, muthafuckin' Jiffy corn bread. Ummm-hmmm! Then I chased that muthafucka with a big ol' glass of yo' Kool-Aid, bitch-ass nigga!" C-Black seriously stated.

Sparks were flying from Kane's dreads as he held the phone to his ear.

"Can you hear me now? What's wrong, tough guy? Cat got your tongue? We know what got hers!"

Kane hung up the phone, then dialed Diamond's number.

"Hey, baby. What' up?" Diamond answered.

"Nothin' much. C-Black over there?"

"Yeah, he downstairs eating with his greedy ass! That fool acting like a straight refugee. Where you find him . . . in Haiti?"

Kane figured out the nigga's game. *It's on now*, he considered.

"Look, baby. That nigga was a ho in the penitentiary. So, whatever he eats out of, let him keep it, feel me?"

"What you mean a ho, baby?"

"He was a nigga girlfriend in the penitentiary," Kane lied.

"Boy, why you didn't tell me this? I would've took them paper plates and utensils out. Shit, Kane. I just bought that damn china! You don't think he's got that gangsta, huh?"

"Can't be too careful, or sure. Just do me a favor. He won't trip; he may even be used to it."

"What's that, baby?" Diamond considered.

"Put the plate and the silverware in a bag, then give it to him when he leaves, okay?"

"No problem. That's it?"

"That's it, li'l mama."

"When you get back, I feel like going to catch a movie tonight."

"I have one more stop; then I'll be home shortly afterward. Love ya, baby."

Click.

Kane suddenly was receiving an incoming text message from a familiar number:

We're having a baby.
Love, Tara.

Everything got dark to Kane as he was driving along the interstate. His mind was running rampant, considering the blow he was just dealt. He'd been having unprotected sex with Tara on the strength of her being a good girl with a bright future. She didn't hang in the hood, nor have any dealings with hood niggas. But now wasn't the time for this type of drama. He had who he wanted. But what would Diamond say about this? He vowed not to let that happen. So he called Tara.

"Hey, baby it's been three months since I've seen you. What are you doing?" Tara inquired.

"The same ol' shit, getting situated. So, how long have you known about this pregnancy?"

"Right before you left. But it was a spur of the moment, so there was no chance to say what needed to be said," Tara reasoned.

"Thought you were on birth control."

"I thought I was too. Guess the patch is not a hundred percent effective. The baby is due in February next year, and you'd better be here, in light of your situation," Tara insisted.

Kane was at a loss for words. But he knew he couldn't encourage her to kill the baby. She wasn't built like that and was raised to know and understand that God didn't make any mistakes. *If this baby made it through the many odds it took in getting here, surely that chance to live life shouldn't be cut short for no reason*, he considered.

"I'll be there, sweetie. Are you still good down there?" he inquired. He knew she would need new clothing for her and the baby, and he needed to provide it.

"Not really, 'cause there's going to be some major changes in a few months with my body, as you know. A little help would be needed, but I'm independent. So you know ain't no nigga going to be feeding this baby but the daddy," Tara promised.

"That's good to hear, sweetheart. I know how you're rocking. The thought of you misrepresenting yourself never crossed my mind. Look, be looking for a wire transfer into your bank account. I'm in motion with a lot of things, but I'll be dropping in on you a little more frequently, okay?"

"You know I love you, right?" she asked Kane.

"Never doubted that for a second."

"Then, you be safe, 'cause that feeling remains and are my concerns. You know these streets be speaking of some ugly shit at times," she offered.

"You got that, li'l mama. Just don't get all mushy on me. Stand tall like I know you will. You know my line of work, and I do it very well," Kane added. "I'll always be a step ahead of the streets because the gossip and the guesses always come before the real. You just do you and fuck the rest. Now, you stay strong and don't worry about nothing but staying healthy," Kane instructed.

The two hung up.

Tara lay in bed pondering the startling information she'd just heard from her cousin, Ray-Ray. She and Ray-Ray grew close since he came home from doing a bid in Parchman Penitentiary. He never came over to her house until recently, but they talked daily about family matters in particular, and of life. Now he was headed out of town on business, he told her. However, she overheard him speak of returning with Kane to face execution for what he did to some powerful people.

Her heart was thumping as if it wanted to jump out of her chest. This was a hell of a dilemma. Blood versus love. She knew it wouldn't be her place to tell one about the other. *That would be betrayal! It's the life they both lived, so there were bound to be clashes*, she told herself.

Damn! How'd I just happen to walk in on that conversation? Maybe I was supposed to hear it, she pondered. *Did I do the right thing by not interfering? Would they have listened if I tried to form a truce between them?* Then she asked herself the ultimate question. *If one of them gets killed, would it feel like I pulled the trigger?*

Chapter 13

Doctor Chowu, Doctor Gore, and Doctor Sanja all were at the school site in the Ninth Ward, overseeing the project. James had allocated each school a budget of five million apiece, well over what was needed. However, the schools were to be built to the scientists' exact specifications. Who better to know what the school's design should be than the men behind the technologies being taught? James had calculated.

"Everything is coming along nicely," Doctor Chowu commented.

"Who would've thought," Doctor Gore said, "five years ago, we'd be on the brink of history? I mean, groundbreaking history, years later? I know it's a hell of an accomplishment, but it's been the farthest thing from my mind because of what's going on with James," Doctor Gore expressed.

"That's so true," Doctor Sanja said. "The gratification I received in being a part of this experience had everything to do with the man who brought us together. His contribution to this work meant just as much as ours. He should be a part of this process!"

"But he's not," Doctor Chowu cued in. "He's lying up in some hospital, fighting for his life because he chose to fight for those who could not fight for themselves. Nevertheless, he left us in charge in case he didn't make it to see this thing through. He believed in us from the beginning, and now in the end. We must see this thing through, no matter what," Doctor Chowu encouraged them.

"I think James left all us packages with contact info to his family and the banks, right?" Doctor Sonja inquired.

Both men nodded.

"Then, I think it's time we introduce ourselves so that we can get the recruiting drives in full gear. I've been getting crazy e-mails from old college buddies wanting in on the possibility of becoming professors at the schools," Doctor Sanja expressed.

"I've gotten a few inquiries from my old professors wanting in on this new technology too," Doctor Gore said.

"My, my. This technology has many driven people excited and aching for a piece of the action. I can honestly say that if it were me in their position, I'd be doing the same. Why not? It's the future," Doctor Gore stated.

"Exactly, and we must deliver it as expected. So, when our friend awakens, he'll know his life's work is a work in progress," Doctor Chowu concluded.

Suddenly, the scientists all boarded a Johnson Industries company vehicle as they prepared to visit their next school. Doctor Chowu retrieved his cell phone, opened the portfolio James provided him, then dialed a number from within it.

"Hello?" Troy answered.

"Yes, I'm calling for a Mr. Troy Johnson."

"Speaking," Troy acknowledged.

"Yes, Troy. This is Doctor Chowu. I've just left the school site under construction. My colleagues and I have some critical matters we'd like to discuss with you at your earliest convenience."

"That's fine. I actually was about to contact you and the others," Troy replied.

"Well, it seems we're right on time. If possible, we'd like to meet immediately."

"That's exactly what I thought before you called. I think great minds think alike," Troy joked. "Is it possible for you to get the other scientists together, then meet me on Canal Street at our law firm?"

"Coincidently, the others are with me now, and we're headed your way."

"I'll be here when you arrive, then," Troy said. "But my sister won't. She's still in the hospital."

"I'm very sorry to hear that, Mr. Johnson. However, I didn't see anything in my package from James concerning your sister's role, with all due respect, of course. It's just that James stated that the fewer people directly involved with the projects was better."

"You're right, Doctor. But as you know, James isn't with us right now, and my sister will be in a day or two. It won't get any closer than us. Also, the decision has been made to use the law firm as Johnson Industries headquarters instead of hiring a firm to do what we already know how to do. So, Deon will assume the role of Public Relations Executive in charge of the company's image. Who better to do that than her?" Troy inquired.

"That's quite extraordinary, Mr. Johnson. I see

intelligence runs in the family. That makes me more eager to meet Ms. Johnson too," Doctor Chowu said.

"Trust me, Doc, she's brilliant if you think I'm smart. Thanks for the compliment. But I mustn't take credit for us coming together in a crisis. It was the only logical move that made any sense. James thought out everything to the tee. All I'm doing is supplying the legwork. Also, while I'm on that subject, we have some major security concerns to address."

"We're pulling into the parking lot on the side of the firm now," Doctor Chowu stated.

"Okay, just have a seat in the lobby. I'm coming to get you," Troy said, then hung up.

Troy was leaving the office when he received a text from Deon: I'm on my way home! "How'd she pull that off?" Troy pondered.

He rode the elevator down, thinking about his recent conversation with Maria. He noticed his reflection from the brass-plated walls within the elevator. The thought of Maria brought a smile to his face. He straightened his tie and then thought, *Damn, I've come a long way since my incarceration in Angola. Let's keep it that way.* The door opened; then he strolled into the lobby.

"Gentlemen," Troy greeted, extending his hand. "It's nice to meet you."

One at a time, the men introduced themselves, shook hands, then boarded the elevator.

"James kept you guys a secret from me for a very long

time, but I do understand him a bit more every day since he's been gone. His meticulous preparation has enabled us to continue functioning," Troy reminded the scientists as they exited the elevator.

"Your brother is truly a gifted man, and I think I speak for all of us on this project; it is a pleasure to work for him," Doctor Chowu declared.

The other two scientists nodded in agreement.

"However," Troy began, "James held a meeting with the family before this tragic incident." He now held his office door open as the scientists all walked into the spacious office. "Can I offer you gentlemen anything before I continue?" He walked over to the small minibar and refrigerator.

"Just water for me," Doctor Gore stated.

"Us, too."

Troy passed the water bottles down the line, then took a seat behind his desk.

"Gentlemen, as I was saying earlier about James's meeting. He stressed the importance of extra security once this idea was introduced. Having said that, I think you guys' knowledge need to be protected at all costs. Think about it. Who would be the next likely targets?"

The scientists looked at each other, understanding Troy's point.

Troy continued. "These technologies have been patented but not taught yet. And you can best believe the enemies understand this also. It's evident that whoever attacked our family will stop at nothing short of destroying any efforts by us to introduce this technology to the

world. And we do understand that they don't mind killing in the process. So we must defend ourselves," Troy
emphasized.

"What are you suggesting, Troy?" Doctor Sanja
inquired.

"I know you gentlemen don't take too kindly about
your privacy being invaded but trust me, you'll thank me
in the end. Once everything is in motion, then everything
goes back to normal," Troy assured them.

"We've prepared to move you as well as your families to gated communities and to add twenty-four-hour
security. This means being chauffeured to and fro with
personal bodyguards. If you think you're not in that
much danger, think of James! He had security like the
Secret Service at his mansion — and look what occurred.
It looks like you guys are the last of the Mohicans," Troy
concluded.

"This will truly be an inconvenience for all our families, but the concerns by far outweigh the personal incon-
veniences. I feel we've come too far to turn around, Troy.
Let's do this," Doctor Gore agreed.

"Very good," Troy stated. "We have some homes that
we've selected that you men can view with your family.
But the security starts today. The company we've used
since our existence is trained by the best and is the best
available. If they say lie down and roll over, do as they
say. These men will take a bullet for you so that you won't
have to. That favorite car you love so much will be replaced with armored ones driven by your security. This
will only be temporary, but it's not a joke, gentlemen. It's

closer to a bad dream if you take the magnitude of this project lightly.

"Any more questions before we move on to recruiting staff and student enrollments, advertising, etc.?" Troy inquired, then took off his navy-blue jacket, slung it across the back of the chair, and started rolling up his sleeves.

All the scientists remained silent as Troy produced a video disc from his briefcase that held the presentations and commercials for Johnson Industries. James had hired a company by the name of Creative Innovations to shoot the ads, as well as print brochures for advertisements.

Through binoculars, the three scientists were being watched. The gentleman across the street in the blue Crown Victoria had been on their trail the whole day. Whatever they did or wherever they went was being documented and photographed. His name was Joseph Breaux, a local private investigator hired by someone with deep pockets who gave only a number where he could be reached. Nothing else would be needed, either. At two hundred dollars an hour in a recession, Joseph didn't ask too many questions. That would only drive business away, and that was ridiculous!

This particular client wanted specifics about each scientist. What they drove, the places they visited, and which one was the leader. A lazy man's dream, Joseph figured, then started snapping more pictures.

Now Joseph was seated outside of Johnson Industries,

placing a call to the unknown person who hired him. The phone went directly to voice message.

Beep.

Joseph began, "I don't know if this means much, if anything, but your three scientists have been inside a law firm by the name of Johnson & Johnson for an hour." He then hung up, feeling like maybe he'd left some valuable information.

"Charles Daniels, pack your shit," the sergeant at Camp-C yelled to Dirty, who was good friends with Kane, as he stood talking to his big homie, Trueblood.

"Ain't nothing to pack, Sergeant. I'm leaving with nothing but what I have on," Dirty assured him.

"Man, you stay out there," Trueblood encouraged.

The two men had been childhood friends. Kane came along later, but they were all real close. They all met in Angola, then hung like wet clothes. Dirty had just finished a fifteen-year sentence, having served eight years, and would be on parole for the final seven. Kane entered Angola with five years, and Trueblood with twenty-five. All from Jefferson Parish, home of the most racist, unethical, and arrogant judicial system in the country. Not only did they have the highest conviction rate, but they also have the highest overturn rate. Meaning, the higher courts find more illegal conduct by prosecutors and judges that overturn criminal convictions of prisoners than any other judicial system in America. The bottom line was, Jefferson Parish lives up to its name: Hang a Nigga, U.S.A.!

"You just hold it down out there, playa. I'm a hop, skip, and jump away," Trueblood assured him.

"I got you, big brother, like a cow got milk, and that's my word! Everything you could ever wish for will be waiting for you when you get there," Dirty promised. "But you make sure you make it out of this place safe, homie. There are still haters walking around here, anticipating a slipup from a real nigga so that they can capitalize on it, feel me?"

"Oh yeah. That's fo' sho'. Just as the sun gon' rise, so will a hater," Trueblood admitted. "That's why I stay clutching that tool. Damn, man. All the niggas we done laid down in here, you'd think the picture was clearer than our first."

"I guess not. But the last time I checked, Administration was still clearing out land at Point Lookout Cemetery. They must be anticipating more of our work."

"That must mean them haters have our names in their mouths again," Trueblood offered. "You know I'm not trying to do no changing. So it's going to be some sad singing and flower bringing around this penitentiary real soon!"

"Rock on with yo' bad self," Dirty encouraged. "I hear this nigga Dip out there interfering with the motion of the ocean," Dirty stated as a matter-of-fact. "So, me and Kane have some shit to clean up too. Other than that, I'ma get this paper like a real nigga 'pose to," Dirty promised. As the two men dapped off, steady talking shit, they reminisced about the past, present, and future. "Oh yeah. Them boys Troy and Luqman been getting loose as a muthafucka too in New Orleans, like they own that bitch. But it's time they recognize my street credibility and kick out like them slot machines in Harrah's Casinos, feel that?" Dirty questioned.

"Like a beach full of naked models," Trueblood stated, then gave Dirty a fist pound.

"Look, I don't give a fuck who his brother is. That only means I'll have eight pockets to dig in to get his money instead of four! Oh yeah, them fools gon' respect my gangsta, 'cause I intend to hit them streets like the plague and take no prisoners — only propositions and positions," Dirty promised.

"Charles, get yo' ass down that walk!" Sergeant Mansion yelled out loud. "Boy, you act like you don't want to leave, all that damn crying you did while you were here."

Dirty's head twisted toward the sergeant, and his eyes told a story of pure hatred. For thirty seconds, he just stared, then stated, "You're right, old man. I did cry twice. Once when I lost my mother, and once when you fuckin' heroes made it to that snitch rescue before I could kill his bitch ass!"

"That's right, Charles. I Tasered yo' ass real good that day. Only so you'd be able to walk out of this penitentiary one day," Sergeant Mansion stated.

"You did that. I agree with you, Sergeant Mansion. But have I thanked you for it yet?" Dirty asked.

"Nope."

"And I never will either! You see, there's only one regret I leave here with today, Sergeant. I regret that even though I've stalked you like a predator ever since you dipped in my business, I never got the opportunity to torture and then kill you without anyone being around."

"Do you really mean that?" Sergeant Mansion asked.

"What the fuck you think, pig?" Dirty asked with a side-eyed look.

Dirty smiled an evil grin as he witnessed the look of concern on the officer's face. "So watch your back, muthafucka!"

Dirty then threw up the peace sign to his homeboy, Trueblood, then walked out of the dorm.

Trueblood shook his head at the young man that entered the penitentiary a boy . . . and was now leaving a beast! One thing he knew for sure. The streets were due for some major changes once Dirty made it out there to them. Simply put, that nigga strolling down that walk toward his freedom was one low-down muthafucka!

Chapter 14

The meeting was called by Saul Deblanco, the head of the notorious Cali Cartel. The limos, Aston Martins and Bentleys, all were arriving at the security gates of Saul's mansion. Every person present at the meeting represented a portion of territory in California except one man, Donovan Silva.

Donovan met Saul while doing time at Rikers Island for drug trafficking. Donovan's identity had been changed through cosmetic surgery that altered everything from his facial features to his fingerprints prior to him doing time at Rikers. His new identity reported that he was from the Dominican Republic.

While at Rikers, Saul and Donovan both were as vicious as any men at the prison. Sometimes, it would seem that they were running a race, considering the bloodshed they were causing on opposite sides of the prison.

However, they developed a respect for the other's business dealings once they met face-to-face and had the chance to assess their similarities. From that moment, they formed an alliance instantly as both men also had major connections in the drug world.

Saul was the head of the Cali Cartel that wreaked havoc on the streets of Los Angeles since the days Saul's uncle headed the cartel in the eighties.

Once both men were discharged, they formed an alliance that trafficked drugs from the Eastern to the Western Hemisphere that netted the men fortunes. The state of California had never experienced the bloodshed and political restructuring that was implemented by the heavy hands of Saul Deblanco. The get down or lay down laws were being carried out on politicians, judges, and the streets. Territories were virtually being abandoned in anticipation of Saul's interest in them. Life was grand for the two men and the few who decided to get down . . . rather than lie down.

However, tonight's meeting would be about the threat of them losing in a game that they had always won.

The five men who represented territories throughout California were comfortably seated and positioned at the round table. Saul began thanking everyone for coming on such short notice and then expressed the urgency of their meeting as the basis of the short notice. He spoke to the men with an air of power, intelligence, and respect. Donovan was seated in the shadows of the room as he always did, observing everyone, saying nothing in his trademark Versace shades. He too wondered what tonight's meeting would bring.

"Today, gentlemen, we're faced with an untimely problem of a certain 'inventor' of sorts. This individual has threatened to render our mass distribution of cocaine and heroin nonexistent." Saul stared at the men around the room for emphasis. "He claims to have discovered a way to turn our drugs into alternate fuel that would power these new vehicles also designed by his company.

That, my friends, must not happen!" Saul banged his fist on the table as he finished the statement.

"I've had major problems already in obtaining any amount of drugs from my connect overseas for any amount of money. I've virtually been on the phone the entire last week trying to persuade anyone from Cuba to Colombia to sell. The same name keeps popping up every time. James Johnson! This damn James Johnson has dealt us some critical blows in the way we do business."

"What are our options?" asked Clemente Garcia.

"We only have one, and I'm not sure how long it will take. But one thing is for sure . . . Sitting around waiting for our empires to crumble *isn't* an option. We must attempt to derail this idea, and we must do it very quickly," Saul recommended.

"I heard the Saudis already tried that," stated Hector Satorie.

"Thanks for the military lesson, Mr. Satorie. And yes, they tried, but *we'll* succeed where they have failed," Saul shot back.

"What's more interesting," Hector began, "is that within hours of the attempted assassination on Mr. Johnson's life, three Saudi oil princes arrived in separate countries that supply drugs to the world. They have not been heard from since. No doubt, they tried to negotiate over Mr. Johnson. Then King Khalid's palace in Saudi Arabia was invaded, and he was assassinated within hours of the attempt on Mr. Johnson's life." Hector paused for emphasis, then continued. "Furthermore, the king's security had managed to capture one of the assassins, but

while being interrogated at a Saudi prison, the lone assassin was then rescued by none other than America's
most wanted, Osama bin Laden," Hector concluded.

The men in the room were now feeling uncomfortable about challenging James. On the other hand, Saul
was pissed.

"Very good, Mr. Satorie," Saul said, unconvincingly.
"You make it seem like we're dealing with superheroes,"
he angrily suggested.

"Just stating the facts, Saul . . . unless you've heard
something different?"

The eyes of all the men at the table shifted toward
Saul, awaiting his reply. About twenty seconds passed
without an answer, so Hector continued.

"Look, Saul. I too have been monitoring this situation. Fuck, I'm too young to retire, and I damn sure never
figured I'd be forced to. We simply don't have the lever-
age we need. Sure, we can travel down the same road as
the Saudis, then expect different results, or we can figure
out a way around it! What the heck. We have plenty of
money. Maybe we can be a part of this new market. I
mean, stopping it seems far-fetched!"

"So, how about we do both?" Saul replied. "It's possible we can attempt to derail it *and* get on board. Then, if
we fail in one, we succeed in the other."

Hector shrugged. He knew separation from any operation against James would be very healthy for him and
unhealthy for whoever didn't; history had already revealed that truth.

Saul walked over to the video equipment, then

inserted a disc. He dimmed the lights and began speaking about the facts that appeared from the surveillance footage.

"Gentlemen, Johnson Industries is owned and operated by this man, James Johnson. But at the present time, he's laid up in a hospital with bullet wounds and remains in a coma. The assassins did a pretty good job on him, his sister, and relatively nothing to his brother."

Suddenly, all three faces of the Johnson family clan appeared on the screen.

Donovan slid to the front of his chair, from his once-relaxed position, then removed his shades as Saul continued to speak. But Donovan didn't hear a word as his focus continued to be on the screen. There was no mistaking it. The three individuals on that screen Saul was plotting to kill were indeed his kids!

Wayne Johnson had hoped this day would—and would not—come. In his mind, he figured it to be too risky. Then, there was just too much heart and pain associated with a reunion.

But he knew his friend, Tray, would do what was best for them, he considered as he thought about the success of Johnson Industries. He now wondered a million things about his family after seeing them for the first time in fifteen years. However, the billion-dollar question he was now faced with involved which of the families he would choose? As a father, there was an obligation like no other to protect his children. But he was a different person now. He hadn't been a father in a very long time.

Saul continued. "This is our time to strike and strike

hard! We must send a message to not only these three but to the world. You fuck with the Cali Cartel and our affairs — we wipe you off the map!"

"Sounds like it's going to be easy," Hector said sarcastically.

"It also sounds like you've become very disrespectful lately," Saul insinuated.

"I'm just speaking the truth, Saul," Hector offered.

"Fuck your truth," Donovan interjected. "I've listened to you rave about this muthafucka, James Johnson as if he's an action hero. But can you explain to me why he's laid up in a fuckin' hospital bed riddled with bullets?" Donovan asked as he walked over to Hector, invading his space.

Hector shrugged.

"Saul, how the fuck do you want to do this?" Donovan asked.

"It's about time someone with some balls showed up," Saul stated, looking around the room. "I want to wipe them black muthafuckas off the face of this earth!"

"Okay, gentlemen. There's the call," Donovan insisted. "Anyone have a problem, this would be the time to say something," he stated aggressively.

No one said a word.

"Very well, Saul. Continue formulating your plan," Donovan said, then took a seat in the corner.

"I want his entire family destroyed, gentlemen. If we can't get to him, get to his mother, his father, and siblings," Saul demanded.

Donovan sat in the corner unmoved by the talk of

destroying the Johnson clan. For a moment, the mentioning of killing his wife, Bertha, didn't resonate. He showed no emotion—the life he lived on the run from his past called for none.

"Donovan," Saul called, jarring him out of his deep thought.

"What's up, Saul?"

"I need you to take a trip to oversee the slaughter."

"No problem. I'll leave shortly," Donovan assured him.

And just like that, Donovan Silva was tasked with destroying the family he ultimately sacrificed his identity for. His new life had turned him into a monster—and the sadistic part about it was that he enjoyed it, even looked forward to it.

Chapter 15

Everybody inside of Julio's gambling shack was having a wonderful time as the free drinks and food that consisted of fried chicken, baked macaroni, barbecue ribs, fish, and potato salad made them feel right at home. There was even a live band playing any request for a small fee. "Down-Home Blues," "Cherish the Love," and "Happy Feelings" were requested all night. The band made a killing, and the proceeds supplied the members' heroin habits, as usual.

The scent of expensive cigars, cigarettes, and Granddaddy Purp flowed through the air and lungs of the gamblers as they chased that mighty dollar all night long. Everything was love, and no guns were allowed unless you were security. All the big ballers were in attendance: Big Mike, C-Lo Green, Tree Top, Pokey, and Li'l Lang, just to name a few. Every man mentioned was a seven-figure player, with more money than they knew they had. There was a hundred-thousand-dollar ante just to make it past the doorjamb, and the dress code was strictly enforced. NO SHORTS! Crap tables were being faded at a thousand dollars a shot.

Julio strolled around the shack like Hugh Heffner at the Playboy Bunny Ranch. He didn't have a care in the world. *Life is sweet*, he thought.

That's how the game is played, Shaky thought. *It's not ratting; it's getting out first.*

Agent John Cage smiled exceedingly, like a cat in a fish market while seated in the back of the SWAT truck. For some reason, he figured this bust would bring him one step closer to bringing down the Johnson clan. He possessed the command of fifty federal, state, and local law enforcement officers, two K-9 units, the authority to rip the place apart and seize all ill-gotten gains. Basically, anything that wasn't nailed down could be confiscated and put in the possession of "Julio" John schemed as he said the name aloud.

A perimeter was being set up around the shack so that no one could enter and definitely not leave, other than authorities. John gave the signal for the first wave of men to get in position to knock down the entrance door. Once in position, he gave the signal for the entire force to move in on the gambling shack. "Move, move, move!" he yelled through the radio. The first wave of men moved in with a battering ram and knocked down the door to the entrance as if it were a sheet of paper. The remaining agents moved into the shack like flies on a piece of fresh shit. They had their guns drawn looking for some action as they yelled, "EVERYONE GET THE FUCK DOWN WITH YOUR HANDS BEHIND YOUR HEAD!"

John strolled in like Elliot Ness observing everything, yet not surprised to see all the money scattered everywhere. The scent of drugs burning was so thick, even the air couldn't pass a piss test. The K-9s were on their job, sniffing out all the drugs that were thrown down on the floor by the convicted felons and parolees, once they realized the po-pos had invited themselves to the party.

Julio was seated in the corner, watching everything, but saying nothing as if he didn't speak English while the agents were handcuffing him, preparing him for his trip to the paddy wagon outside.

"Julio, my man. What's goin' on? Long time no see," John stated as he walked over to Julio and took a seat.

Who is this cocksucker? I don't know any pigs, Julio thought as he ignored John.

"What's the matter, cat got your tongue?" John joked. "Trust me, I can understand why. For instance, being that all the drugs and money we find will belong to you, I'd expect that you would want to speak to a lawyer instead."

"A lawyer for what? You don't have anything on me," Julio boasted.

"So, you're not the owner of this fine establishment?" John stated sarcastically as he looked around.

"Naah. Not today anyway. Right game, Officer, but the wrong guy."

"Well, would you happened to know who owns this place?"

"Don't really matter to me, Officer. I'm just buying a chicken plate. Who owns the kitchen don't matter to me."

"Sounds like you got it all figured out. Guess you're a master of elaborate escapes," John joked as the other agents laughed. Julio just shrugged it off. "I guess you'll be invoking your Fifth Amendment right to remain silent, 'ey, amigo?" John tossed in the air. He stood and began searching Julio, pulling a wallet with identification out of his pocket. "Says here your name is Paul Cassidy. Hmmm, do you strike me as a Paul?" John questioned. His forehead wrinkled as he struggled with the name for jokes, knowing that the ID was fake. "Okay, let's just say you're this Paul muthafucka. Cool. Then you're the one we've been looking for, my man. Actually, this establishment just so happens to belong to Paul Cassidy," John concluded while patting Julio's shoulder.

Julio suddenly brandished a look of concern across his face. He wasn't trippin' on the small amount of drugs and money scattered about the floor. His concern was based on the drug packaging facility underneath the floor. The dogs were going crazy barking and scratching at the floor. He had to do something . . . but what?

"Well, if you got everything figured out, then why am I not being booked on whatever it is that you think you have?" he said, trying to expedite the investigation before the room was discovered.

An agent along with a K-9 officer approached John whispering. A smile appeared on his face; then he nodded as if to say yes to something. The officers left with more spring in their steps than they'd come with before. John turned and faced Julio with a big grin planted across his face.

Trouble, Julio considered.

"Sorry for the interruption, Mr. Paul. Do you mind if I just call you Julio?"

"Call me what the fuck you want. Just call my lawyer afterward!"

"Ohhh, you want to be a Billy Bad-Ass, huh? Mr. Big-Timer with the Big-Time lawyers," John joked. Julio shrugged, seemingly not concerned. "All right what the heck. I'll let you in on it. It seems as though them K-9s are goin' crazy scratching at them damn floors back there. Shit, the last time they did that we busted up a real sophisticated operation up there in New Jersey. Yeah, those boys up there were reeeeal smart, reeeeal sophisticated. They had built them an underground, air-conditioned, drug-packaging facility. Tell me that's not what we're about to find, Julio."

Damn! Caught red-muthafuckin'-handed, Julio thought.

"I'm waiting, Julio," John stated. "Goddammit, man! You dealers down South are not supposed to be that so-phisticated!" Then John thought to himself "This means he has big connections."

"Look, Julio," John began, "them fellas up in Jersey retained those fancy, high-priced New York lawyers and strolled into the federal courts just like you're figurin' to do. What do you think happened when we kept plaster-ing them stacks of cocaine and heroin on that big plasma screen? Some of the jurors puked when we showed the pictures of kids who overdosed from being strung out on that shit. On top of that, mutilated bodies full of bullet holes, indicators of the problem drug wars are inflicting on the community . . . I'll tell you what happened . . . They all got dinosaur numbers in the federal penitentiary. That means they will *never* get out unless someone digs them out of their graves. Maybe you'll have the sense to avoid that and save yourself a few million on lawyers, you know what I mean?" John said, then winked.

"Yeah, I know what you mean, but you still have the wrong guy. Thanks for the history lesson, though. Yet, that's exactly what it'll remain, his-story," Julio insisted, then spat on John's pants leg for disrespecting him. John shook his head for a second, comfortable with the idea of having Julio in such a tight jam. There was no reason to beat him, although he wanted to. He'd fucked over plenty of men for less. But a taste of a jail cell with no bond attached should feel the same.

He walked away and into a room where about ten agents were just uncovering the trap door that led to the packaging room. As the trap door was opening, the medicinal smell of raw cocaine and heroin crept up the stairwell and into the room like Freddy Kruger. The agents descended the stairs and walked into the drug lab. They rounded up a total of twenty-two kilos, twelve of cocaine and ten of heroin. John Cage was happier than a detective with a murder weapon. After seeing the spoils, he sprinted back up the stairs like "Carl" Lewis en route to Julio.

"You muthafuckas need to hurry up and get me wherever it is I'm supposed to be going!" Li'l Lang exclaimed, mad as a muthafucka that all his money and the two hundred grand he was up would ultimately end up in some crooked cop's pocket.

"Who the fuck you supposed to be, shorty?" Agent Amirez stated.

"I'm the muthafucka you'll see in your nightmares, you fuck with me," Li'l Lang replied.

The agent looked Li'l Lang up and down, then started

to laugh. Li'l Lang stood a whopping five-foot-eight but had a little man complex ten feet tall. "So, you're the nightmare I see, huh?" Agent Amirez inquired.

"If that's who you need me to be," Li'l Lang shot back, mean muggin'.

"So, where's the rest of you?" the agent asked. "The guy in my nightmares is at least six foot tall."

"In your old wrinkled-ass mother's pussy," Li'l Lang came back.

"Daaaaamn, he told yo' pussy ass!" Big Mike said, laughing as if he got hit with laughing gas.

"We'll see who's the pussy when you get to the penitentiary. Them convicts are always interested in some good-looking boys like yourself."

Li'l Lang and Big Mike looked at each other and started laughing until tears flowed down their faces.

"Let me get this straight. We supposed to be scared of the penitentiary, right?" Big Mike asked.

"You tell me, tough guy."

"It's obvious that you're new to this shit, 'cause if you weren't, you'd recognize the true players before you, chump. The penitentiary to us is a fuckin' second home, fool!" Big Mike expressed.

"Wit'cha bitch ass!" Li'l Lang added, in addition to Big Mike's jewels he dropped on the agent. The agent considered all that was said and decided to move on, concluding that he was out of his league and should stick to police work.

John Cage escorted Julio to an unmarked vehicle so he could continue his interrogation.

"Looks like you're goin' down like those Jersey boys. But you know I can help you out, right?"

"I don't need your help. I need for you to get me to wherever you're taking me."

Men and women were being escorted to the paddy wagon that was no doubt headed to central lockup. Julio leaned his head up against the window and drifted off into deep thought about all the kilos of drugs being loaded into vehicles as evidence against him. He then thought about what Tray offered as a reason for his retiring from the game. "A Hustler's Dream," he called it. *What the fuck do I do now?*

"Dirty, please don't hurt me!" Diana begged.

"Bitch, you must've been outta yo' fuckin' mind to think I was gon' forget about yo' trick ass leaving a nigga high and dry."

"Dirty, what was I supposed to do? I couldn't support my damn self!"

"Likely fuckin' story, ho! You sho' ain't waste time gettin' with that nigga Nick, huh?" he asked, then punched her in the face again as she kneeled on the ground.

She screamed as loud as her lungs would allow, but she was simply too far away to be heard. Diana was now on the side of the road of *Almonaster* Boulevard, where there had been more dead bodies discovered than anywhere else in New Orleans, besides the projects. *How did I let this nigga fool me into this car?* she thought.

"You know it didn't just happen like that, Dirty. Give a bitch some credit!" Diana lied.

"Credit? Let me make sho' I'm understandin' you," Dirty began. "I'm out c'here hustlin' 24/7 making sho' we have the best of things. Then I take a fall, and you ride out into the sunset in search of another meal ticket. Somewhere along the way, I missed what you contributed that would somehow entitle you to some credit. You dog-ass ho!"

"That's right, nigga. You did all the hustlin'; that was your choice. Countless nights I lay in bed waiting for yo' ass to get home, praying you made it safely. I guess that don't count for nothing, huh? I begged you to back away from the game while you were ahead!" Dirty just looked at Diana unconcerned. "Better yet, muthafucka, you left me! As smart of a nigga as you were, how could you not see the traps in the game that took so many niggas before you?"

Dirty smacked her again, and she fell again. Then, out of his waistband, he pulled a 10-mm Sig and cocked it, adding a bullet to the chamber.

"Bitch, what I chose to do ain't have nothing to do with what you ended up doin'! You could have jumped ship at any time without question, but you chose to stay. You chose to keep enjoyin' the ride, flossin' designer clothes, pushin' foreign whips, and accepting the expensive gifts. So don't try to take me on no guilt trip. The only trap I didn't see was yours, and that's why ya dog ass will die today," Dirty assured her.

"Nigga, I was born to die. Fuck you! I've done accepted the fact that none of us will leave here alive," Diana bucked, then spat blood from her mouth at Dirty. She knew her time had come, and she'd be damned if she spent the last of it beggin' a nigga who had his mind made up for years. "I feel like you feel, nigga; I had to do what I had to do to survive. That's the law I'm under. All of a sudden, you taking this relationship shit personal like you cared. Pulleeese! Nigga, there are always two users in a relationship. If I didn't have anything you wanted, the next bitch would've had you, and vice versa. Now, after all these years, you come out holding a grudge on a bitch out here tryin' to make it. You know what the real niggas say? Fair exchange ain't no robbery, nigga, so get over it!"

Dirty studied Diana and almost wanted to respect what she was saying, but one thing about a mouth: it'll say anything.

"Yeah, you have a good-ass point there. Them real niggas said a lot of shit!" he expressed. Then his face displayed an evil grin as he prepared his last words before a passerby came along and wanted to play Eyewitness or Last Action Hero. "Them real niggas also said a lady and a bitch can't switch. That was my bad for violating that code. Now, after realizing it, I'm here to set the record straight!"

Then Dirty started pumping lead into Diana's body and head until the clip was empty and the gun barrel smoked. Now satisfied with releasing all the pent-up anger that dwelled inside for so long, Dirty turned to leave, then turned back as if he had forgotten something. He walked over to Diana's body, then kicked it. Satisfied that she was dead, he unzipped his pants and began pissing on the corpse, just as he said he would years ago.

"That golden shower you just received is for when you get to hell and need a glass of water. Bitch! There's your credit. Use it wisely." As he finished, a smirk appeared on his face. He kinda respected the way the bitch went out. Some of the niggas cried like babies, he laughed to himself.

He strolled back to his brand-new BMW 7 Series, hopped in, and pulled off. Tupac was playing in the background. *"I heard it's poppin' at a club, but they said I can't get in 'cause I'm dressed like a thug; until I die I'll be game related."* Dirty was bobbing his head feeling free like an Arab in a desert as he wiped clean the 10-mm pistol, breaking it down, tossing a piece out into the woods every couple of blocks.

It had been an entire week since he'd left the penitentiary, and Dirty was enjoying every minute, flossing the new Beamer, the tricked-out condominium, and the six-figure bank account that Kane laced him up with as a present. His next order of business would be Dip's bitch ass, he now considered. *Wonder what Kane is doing?*

He called Kane, and the phone rang three times before Kane answered.

"What it do, my brotha from a different motha?" Kane asked.

"Ain't shit, playa. Just getting things situated in this city of mines," Dirty claimed.

"Shit, who you don' declared war upon?"

"Anybody that's on my list or in my way. Speaking of which, where this pussy-nigga Dip be at down here?"

"Not sure, but like a man," Kane expressed, "you're

gonna need more than heart to step to dude, homie. What are you in a rush for?"

"You know I treat this shit like a crap game, homie. I'm on a roll, so I gots to fade everybody I said I would," Dirty shot back.

"In due time, my brotha. Look, we're playin' at a whole new level, yo. Killin' is a game of necessity rather than convenience. 'Cause everything is done to either forward or set up our next move," Kane schooled. "Trust me on this matter, Dirty. Patience will keep you safe, rich, and out of the penitentiary."

"I feel ya', bruh, but you know I'm like ready to get this thing crackin' out chere," Dirty reasoned.

"I know exactly who you are and what you're ready to do. But shit must be played through the eyes and minds of wise men if we want to win. Peep this; if the organization we're up against was to hear even a whisper of their names, it's going to be bad for us. We're not dealing with local niggas. These muthafuckas stretch all the way around the world like an elastic band, playboy."

"Who the fuck you talkin' 'bout?"

"The same niggas you inquirin' 'bout!" Kane stressed.

"Them boys doin' big thangs like that?"

"Your imagination couldn't guide you to where them niggas at, my brotha. On everything, I spit the real when it comes to you, Dirty. This program Troy, Dip, and Luqman on will be written about one day. Don't ask me how, but Troy's brother has the world eating out of his hand like zoo animals, and you can take that to the bank. So, if it's war you want, it's whateva with them.

They have everybody and their momma on their side. Politicians, Mafia, drug lords, president, police, military, *and* the streets," Kane concluded.

"And how are you so informed on these super-Negroes?"

"Because I have been working with them for the last three years, and I do my homework."

"Word is that these niggas a threat to you."

"That would be correct, but I'm not goin' to war without an army. These dudes are at full strength, even though they're injured. The wisest thing for us to do is pay attention. I'm on a major come-up with big thangs on the agenda; things that put money in the bank *not* take it out. Wars cost money, so you can't make money and war, son. I know you like them new toys and that cash sittin' in your bank account, right?" Kane asked.

"Oh yeah! You know I do, homie."

"Then act like it and enjoy yourself. Think of some big-money shit you want to explore and let me strategize this war shit before you come up missing."

"Nigga, ain't no fear of death in me!" Dirty snapped back.

"Yeah, right. That shit sound brave but ain't no fear in them killing you either. So, who profits?"

Dirty thought long and hard about Kane's last re-marks. *This nigga gettin' all soft on a playa. Cool, he runnin' the show for now. That weak shit just may get his wig pushed back. Not to mention he talkin' crazy to me.*

"That's exactly what I thought," Kane said.

If you only knew, Dirty thought as he hung up.

Chapter 16

"Hello?" Dip answered.

"Hey, stranger," Akbar replied.

"I thought you left the country."

"Not yet," said Akbar. "Maybe later, though."

"Sounds like you're ready to do some business."

"Exactly," Akbar agreed.

"How much did we agree on?"

"That was then; just wanted to see if you were interested. I have rules now."

"Why is that?"

"It's better for all of us. Plus, it's safer for me."

"Who's all of us?" Dip questioned.

"One second, Dip," Akbar stated. "Hey, Kane. Akbar here, what's good?"

"Is this what you called me for?" Dip said with contempt.

"I called to do business. I'm still in possession of the disc," Akbar stated arrogantly.

"I figured you would be. So where do we go from here?"

"I have new rules to an old game. It will be better for all of us this way."

"All of who?" Kane asked, puzzled.

"Where are my manners?" Akbar said with a bit of sarcasm. "Kane, say hello to Dip. You know him, right?"

There was a silence only broken by the voice of Akbar.

"Okay, fellas, that's not really important. Today, we are going to bid on the disc between the two of you. You both are facing life-and-death sentences because of what's on my disc. So, don't play yourself. Both of you will receive account numbers to an overseas bank. I will need the winning bidder to deposit the money within five hours, or the loser gets the disc for five-hundred-thousand less. I will now start the bidding at five-hundred grand."

"Seven," Dip said.

"Eight," Kane said.

"One million," Dip shot back.

Kane paused a second, knowing his money wasn't as long as Dip's.

"One point five," Kane railed.

"Two million!" Dip free styled.

That was the farthest Kane could go without breaking himself.

"Two million going once. Two million going twice. Sold! Okay, gentlemen, here's a little twist that will conclude the deal. I'm going to make this a fair deal. I'm going to drop the price by five hundred grand, and offer you both the disc for one point five million. Seeing that this is a clear case of big bank takes little bank, this strategy will either make you respect the other or kill him. The choice is yours. Not to mention that I'll be up a million both ways," Akbar said proudly.

"Fair for who?" Dip questioned.

"Stop cryin', nigga," Kane snapped. "What'cha scared of?"

"Notyou!Mr.Get-Outta-Town-With-The-Quickness!"

"Fo' sho'," Kane agreed. "A good run will beat a bad stand any day."

"Betta' keep runnin' 'cause if you stop, gaaame ova'," Dip assured him.

"That, my brotha, remains to be seen. That's only talk, and that don't count in my book!"

"Just keep looking ova' ya shoulder. One day, it'll be me, and, bitch, don't cry!"

"I'll keep that in mind, gurly man," Kane joked.

"ALL RIGHT, FELLAS! Back to business. You each have five hours to complete the transfer. Dip, your number is 76665426. Kane, yours is 6628975. Call me when it's complete and not before. Am I clear?"

"When will I receive my disc?" Dip inquired.

"First things first. As soon as you pay, then I'll let you know when and where to pick up the disc."

"This should put a nice-size dent in yo' pocket, Kane," Dip taunted.

"Naah, dog, I'm still spendin' the money I took from yo' peeps," Kane chuckled.

"He who laughs first don't laugh long."

"He who slips doesn't laugh at all. Happy huntin'."

All three men hung up.

"Did you get the location on them two numbers, Irvin?" Dip asked.

"Give my people a second to process the global system, and I'll have the address wherever they were. They may have been in a car on a cell phone," he replied through the phone lines.

"If so, tell them to track the coordinates, and Google Earth the signal to show exactly what they're driving, on the double," Dip stated.

"That shouldn't be a problem. I'm on it now. Pictures will be available in minutes."

"What's the latest on James since he awakened from the coma?"

"He's doing great. A lot of rehabbing, but Salvator is there with him. So it won't be long before he's back to his old self," Irvin promised.

"That night they ushered him out of the hospital was some real slick shit. We never knew he was awake until you called us."

"We received a tip. Someone suspicious was inquiring about his condition, so we couldn't take any chances. We airlifted him to a state-of-the-art rehab facility. Salvator had been there already rehabbing. The last time I was there, they were planning every minute of the day, so the world is in for something real special."

"That's a scary thought," Dip agreed. "Also, the fortress is almost ready. I never seen a place like that design put together."

"I've seen the blueprint, and it's amazing technology. James will have everything at his fingertips," Irvin considered. "There isn't another like it in the world. He certainly won't have to worry about an assassination attempt while he's in there. How's Deon doing since leaving the hospital?"

"She's been hard at work with public relations for Johnson Industries," Dip replied.

"Yes, I've seen the commercials everywhere I'm traveling. This thing has gotten up off the ground and is running its course."

"That's the idea anyway," Dip assured him. "We're doing our best, considering Luqman left for Cuba, Troy for Colombia, Tray for Mexico, and Jaafar for Afghanistan a month ago."

"How are things going with them?"

"Everything is running real smooth, although there were a few kinks in the beginning. But now, the factories are producing the fuel as planned. Many jobs are being produced, and the drug lords are more than happy to keep selling us all their product."

"What about the production of the new vehicles at the plants over there?"

"Man, you wouldn't believe the demand for these vehicles," Dip replied. "We really need James back at the helm. We're in need of more plants over here. We have a backlog on the sports utility vehicles, luxury sedans, sports coupes, and the list is growing as the advertisement increases," Dip informed him.

"I feel that," Irvin said. "Those are some fine-looking vehicles on the commercials, but that gas mileage is off the charts. Three hundred miles per gallon. That's ridiculous! And even at ten dollars a gallon, they can't compete," Irvin assured.

"That's the plan. To eliminate the next man!"

"I agree, and Johnson Industries is definitely

succeeding in doing just that. So, hopefully, you'll be able to keep up with the demand."

"Oh, we're not finished either," Dip emphasized.

"You must be kidding me. More damage to the industry?"

"Yeah," Dip admitted. "We've begun designing motorbikes too. Once the dust settles, it's on again! I received an e-mail from James. He's going to put the oil industry out of business."

"No shit!" Irvin said.

"It's a war, Irvin, and he's not selling any of the stock to this new technology. Everything that uses oil or gas, James is designing newer and more efficient machines to replace them," Dip stated. "Now, look, Irvin. This is only family information, extremely classified."

"Oh, we're crystal clear, Dip. It's good to know this, 'cause I'm always concerned about his safety. That's my job! James actually has more security than the president."

"I can believe that," Dip assured. "Because the president hasn't locked everything, from Wall Street to y'all street," Dip joked.

"You got that right. They picked the wrong brother this time. I know they wish they hadn't," Irvin laughed. "Hey, I just received that information on those two calls. You around a computer?"

"Fo' sho'. Send it to my address at the firm."

"Here it comes now, Dip. Happy hunting," Irvin said, then hung up.

Located on the outskirts of San Antonio, Texas, is an exclusive rehabilitation center where Salvator and James had been for over a month recuperating together.

Joy was also there with them every step of the way, making sure they ate right and worked out hard. Today, they were on the treadmill, and Joy was pushing them to the limit!

"Damn, James. Where did you say you met this woman?" Salvator inquired.

"It feels like Slaves-R-Us," James stated as the two men continued to pace themselves.

"I'm not the one who's running around the country getting shot up. So get back to work and stop crying, busters," Joy shot back.

"I don't have a problem with that, señorita, but you've taken it to another level," Salvator complained.

"As I've stated, you two geezers must think you're bulletproof. So, since you're not, this is where you end up when you find out differently!"

"I see no geezers here," Salvator stated.

"Look who's talking," Joy joked. "Mr. Get-Rescued-by-Osama-bin-Laden, on camels in the middle of the desert," Joy laughed.

"That's right. I did get rescued by my friend on a camel's back and in the middle of the desert. But I lived to tell the story! There were over a hundred men I stopped from telling a war story," Salvator boasted. "They are no longer with us. How's *that* for a geezer?"

Joy listened, then smiled at Salvator's story and had to give him props.

"Cat got your tongue?" James instigated.

"Don't make me get on you!" she threatened.

"Hmmm. And how would you do that? Was my work recorded? It will be very embarrassing if you shot video, sweetie," James stated.

"Just so you know," he continued, "we're two official muthafuckas! We done stop countin' the battles and wars we've been in. People may think we're invincible, like superheroes!"

"Okay, you two invincibles, get back to work. Break's over," Joy insisted.

"Look, my friend just walked in," Salvator said.

A nurse Salvator had been flirting with since he rolled in on the gurney entered the room to check on him again. She was young, pretty, and her name was Mary.

"Don't make me call child protection on you, geezer," Joy threatened.

Salvator climbed off the treadmill, then walk toward Mary, who was all smiles at the sight of him.

"I wonder what he's telling her. She lit up like a Christmas tree," Joy said.

"Maybe it's not what he told her," James stated.

"Well, he can't do her much good in his condition," Joy joked. "Oh, shut up, James. I'm just having fun!"

"Me too," he laughed. "Let's get out of here. I need to show you what I can do in my condition."

"Oooh, sounds like fun. Let's hurry!"

"Where do you think you're sneaking off too?" Salvator questioned.

"So much for your little war story. Bye-bye."

They walked down the hallway toward James's room, then James noticed the new nurse in the reception area had been eyeing him for some strange reason. The nurse was very unattractive, and that alone brought much emphasis to her presence. That *really* made him notice her noticing him. He simply played as though he hadn't.

"How long you think before I'm able to leave this place?" he asked.

"You're recovering really fast, sweetie. Why do you ask?" Joy replied.

"Because I'm planning to unveil the first vehicles in a grand fashion. I want the entire world to witness what the future will look like, and I plan on being there. Also, I have a personal vehicle I am introducing, and the world will stand in awe over it for many years to come."

"In that case, I'll give you two to three weeks tops, especially at the pace we're working."

"That's perfect timing," he considered.

They finally made it to his room, which was a presidential suite by any five-star hotel's standards. Hand in hand, they strolled into the spacious room, then James locked the door behind them as they begin kissing and rubbing noses together in a show of affection. Slowly, they undressed each other. James began peeling off Joy's sweatpants, then sweatshirt, leaving her in only a hot-pink panty and bra set. Joy slid his sweatshirt over his head, then aggressively snatched his sweatpants down, leaving him with only a jockstrap visible. Joy's breathing increased as the anticipated excitement of sexual intercourse dominated her thought processes. Her eyes stayed focused on James's large penis protruding from the jockstrap.

"My, my. Looks like our friend wants out of there," Joy smiled as she ran her fingernail up and down the jockstrap.

"I know he most definitely wants in," James assured her.

"Then, that's what he'll get, then," Joy promised, then strolled over to the huge shower, leaving her bra and panties in her tracks.

Once inside, she adjusted the water to a lukewarm temperature, adjusted the showerhead to a soft sprinkle-massage flow, like she had done so many times before. Then James casually walked into the shower room, admiring Joy's caramel, silky smooth skin, as the water danced along her body. Her long black hair, golden complexion, and Asian eyes made her look like an exotic goddess.

Standing under the showerhead, she turned toward James's six foot four magnificent body with shoulder-length dreads until she shivered at the sight of him approaching her. His eyes were the color of her skin and portrayed the illusion that he was as gentle as a lamb. Yet, she knew better. She knew the viciousness this unique specimen was capable of. However, she also knew his heart, and that's what mattered most!

Her heart rate increased as he closed the distance between them, resembling the African king he is. His muscles flexed with each stride. She felt as if she'd collapse if he didn't hurry, as the soft, warm water cascaded down her body and between her legs, tickling her clitoris.

James placed both of his hands on the wall above Joy, then slid his tongue into her mouth as they passionately kissed. She gently massaged his body, then stroked his manhood. As it grew, the more turned on Joy became, until she couldn't take another second of it. She dropped to her knees and began to give him head. The combination of the water rolling down his nuts and Joy's spectacular head job had James in another time zone. It made him feel like royalty. Then, she began massaging and sucking his nut sac until he felt a familiar tingle. The erection was like no other as he felt the come slowly creep up, threatening to explode.

Joy could now taste the precome, and it made her take James's manhood into her mouth even deeper. She tickled the head of his penis with her tongue in a circular motion as she felt it throb. Anticipating what was about to happen, she grabbed James's body pulling him close, as she bobbed her head up and down until he exploded into her mouth. She then slowly stood up, now satisfied with relieving James from the bodily tension once present.

They both were now under the water, soaping each other as each carefully explored the other's body. Once they rinsed off, James laid Joy down inside the massive shower as the water rained down on them from behind. He began to nibble on her pretty nipples that were harder than a child molester at a kid's concert. Her pussy throbbed as James's massive body straddled hers. He sucked, then kissed her from head to toe. Joy screamed out loud from the ecstasy as James inserted only a couple of inches of his penis into her while he continued paying attention to her toes. She aggressively tried to scoot her body up so more of him would go into her, but he'd blocked her with his knees, anticipating the agony it would cause her. Joy's pussy was throbbing and pushing out orgasm after orgasm as James slowly did his thing.

He positioned her legs in the air, now licking between her thighs. The water was slowly trickling down from the showerhead, and it made her feel like they were underneath a waterfall. James pulled out of Joy, raised her legs high in the air, opened them far apart, then ran his tongue in and around her pussy. She again screamed as another orgasm made her body shake violently.

Now holding her body with all his strength, he continued pleasing Joy with his tongue. She moved her head from side to side as if she were saying no, but he knew she was really saying yes.

"Oh, please! James, stop! Please, baby, please!" Joy insisted.

James continued sucking her clit and felt he'd won the first round. He smiled. In a minute, she would get a taste of his pound game for the second round.

He slid back, then entered her tight pussy with his nine and a half inches stroking long and stroking hard like the Mandingo warrior he is. Joy cried out from the ecstasy and realized she was no longer in control of her life. Her new purpose was only to please James. Tears ran down her face and into her hair.

How did I get myself into this situation? she thought. She had never experienced lovemaking like this before. Never figured it existed.

"Ohhh, James. I'm coming! I'm coming!" she excitedly screamed as they both collapsed in each other's arms.

She thought she loved her job, and that's primarily why she took this assignment in the first place. FBI Agent Joy Turner thought she was getting rid of the bad guys. What was she going to tell Agent John Cage when she reported to him? How could she tell James what would most likely cause her to lose him . . . and possibly her career too?

Chapter 17

Don Santos stood gazing out into the ocean from the balcony of his beachfront mansion, built overlooking the Gulf of Mexico. He'd been thinking about how things had been changing over the last three months since James revealed his plan. There seemed to be less bloodshed over the lack of drugs on the streets, most likely due to the gangs controlling the trade. He was grateful for that. Gangs tended to follow one leader, and if the leader couldn't obtain drugs, the entire territory suffered.

However, the states without cartels or gangs had independent dealers that numbered in the thousands. *That will complicate things*, the don considered. This obligated him to go after these individuals to fulfill his contract with James. But what had to be done was business, and there was no turning back now.

Saul Deblanco, of the Cali Cartel, had contacted him to obtain a large quantity of drugs a month ago. But there was no way in hell that deal would ever happen, even as a favor, Santos concluded.

But desperate times call for desperate measures. The two men never liked each other but respected the other on the strength of their affiliations.

Now, James's plan was unfolding just as he warned them. Don Santos received ten million a month and hadn't touched drugs since, thanks to James. He was now disappointed and relieved at the information coming from the other states under his control.

The killing by his death squad was continuing to drip in daily. In Washington, there were ten deaths, Missouri had eight, Indiana had twelve deaths, and Arkansas topped the list with sixteen.

"Why don't these so-called drug dealers learn to take heed to my warnings about continuing to sell drugs in my state?" he questioned.

Senseless but necessary, his friend Don Giodana expressed to him moments earlier.

Don Santos had lived a productive life at age sixty-five. However, these new endeavors and times were weighing on him. He was used to the old ways. More familiar with liquor, gambling, and politics until drugs became a part of the equation. The core principles that forged alliances suffered severely. Loyalty, respect, and honesty were now replaced by greed, envy, and treachery. Business back then was conducted without contracts, and deals were sealed with a word, and then a man's handshake, the don reminisced. Wars were fought producing many casualties, as any war would. But once drugs hit the scene, senseless destruction of the innocent and guilty manifested. Now, for the first time in his life, he contemplated retirement. *Maybe this plan of James's really could work.*

However, others from within the commission were having open discussions about the power this black man held over them, and it made them rebellious. The Commission had never been ordered around or fed, instead of them possessing the power to feed. That's how they learned the game, and that's what they wanted back!

"Where have you been with your sexy self?" Keoka asked Tray, as he strolled into her business decked out in a Versace shirt, slacks, and sunglasses. Everything black, including the crocs on his feet and diamonds in his ears.

"I've been out of the country, baby. You know I have a job now," he said with a grin.

"Yeah, I see that. It must be modeling, cause you absolutely deserve to be gracing somebody's magazine cover!" she seductively assured him as she stood leaning to one side with her hand on her hip. "So, what brings you to this part of town?" she asked, straightening out a rack of jeans.

"Just passing through, checking on an old friend. Nothing wrong with that, huh?"

"Oh no, baby. It's always a pleasure to lay eyes on you. Since you sold the club, nobody's been able to keep up with you. My baby always asking if you're all right. He'll be home in a couple of months. I'll be very excited when that happens. I'm gon' throw so much pussy on that man, he'll need a wheelchair afterward," she joked.

"That's great news, Keoka. He's just the man I need right about now. Has he been keeping out of trouble?"

"Shit, he better. This system not passing out chances; they passing out death warrants," Keoka joked.

"Right, but I know Brother Wali is for the right things,

and sometimes it gets him in hot water," Tray stated as he watched Keoka straighten up some jewelry in a case.

"He's definitely that. And how long has it been since you and him were pulled over, and he broke that officer's jaw in Jefferson Parish?" Keoka asked.

"About ten years."

"Nine years, eight months, and two days," she corrected him.

"They know what we were trying to do for the community, so they provoked Wali, and he'd had enough. It was time for a stand to be made, and he made it," Tray said.

"Speaking of, I let your protégé into Wali's office the other day."

"And how'd he take it?" Tray asked curiously.

"Mesmerized."

"You reveal anything?"

"Nope. He was speechless for quite some time," she laughed.

"He'll be all right. It's a shocking thing to see the future in one's work today," Tray offered.

"Right, and only if he knew what he was seeing is actually vintage. It's just that the torch isn't being carried with the vigor of an Abdul Wali and yourself."

"So true, yet the younger generation of college students are picking up the protest signs against the establishments of today. And what they don't understand about the movement, Brother Wali will teach them while standing on the front line with them," Tray assured her.

"I think you have a general by your side, Tray."

"We're raising revolutionaries from here on out, Keoka."

"One thing I know for sure is that we have one who'll be here in a few months with his fine ass," she stated, while bent over laughing.

Tray laughed as one of Keoka's customers walked in looking like a tall glass of iced tea to a slave in a cotton field.

"Hey, girl. What's up?" Shawanda asked.

"Nothing, girlfriend. Just kickin' it with my boy, Tray. Tray, this is Shawanda. Shawanda, this Tray."

"The pleasure is all mine, Nubian," Tray responded.

"*Excuse* me?" Shawanda questioned.

"My bad. I was referring to you as a Nubian princess. Don't take it for more than it is. I'm a very happily married man." He showed her an impeccable diamond ring. "I just happen to appreciate beauty and associate it with fine art. I have no problem with reminding a woman of her beauty without an ulterior motive. I think our brothers should remind our sisters of their beauty daily, and sisters should be more accepting. Not all compliments are pickup lines," he said.

"You're exactly right, Mr. Tray. And I don't mind the compliments, especially from a gentleman such as yourself. But most brothers don't know the first thing about how to approach a lady," Shawanda insisted.

"Give them a break, baby," Tray pleaded. "It's not like the schooling they received taught them about proper etiquette, or proper anything for that matter."

Shawanda laughed at the notion of ghetto brothers

and etiquette. "You're not from around here are you?" she asked.

"Actually, not too far. But yes, I've gotten around these parts most of my life."

"Just wondering how I could've missed you."

Tray blushed. Yet, he understood her pain too. "Brothers really need to catch up to the world."

"Keoka, it was good to see you again. But me and Dip have a meeting at the club in a few, so I'll run along. Ms. Shawanda, it's nice to have met you, and if I can help you in any way, here's my card. Don't hesitate."

"I'll keep that in mind. Thanks," she assured him.

"Be safe out there, Tray," Keoka said.

Tray threw up the deuces, then walked out of the boutique, entered his Silver S-Class Mercedes-Benz, and drove off. He glanced at the Presidential Rolex on his wrist, then mashed on the gas as he merged into the interstate at Crowder Boulevard. Two minutes later, he was exiting at Bullard Road, a stone's throw away from the club.

Dip was leaning on his new armor-plated platinum Aston Martin, displaying his muscular frame in a T-shirt and sagging a pair of jeans.

Tray pulled into the spot next to Dip. He exited his Mercedes, then looked around the parking lot, reminiscing.

Club Ballers was a burnt-down building when he purchased it years ago. Now, after he dropped two hundred thousand into its design, there were three floors equipped with separate bars, stripper stages, VIP sections,

DJ booths, picture rooms, and its very own version of the red carpet, called the black carpet. Club Ballers was the first of its kind in New Orleans. Like the Cash Money Millionaires, he raked in no less than a hundred grand every night when performers were onstage.

Tray continued to look around the parking lot, which was the size of a football field.

"Damn, I miss this place!" he stated out loud.

"It misses you too, playboy," Dip replied, giving him a hug and a handshake. "Man, you're looking younger by the day. What's your secret?"

"Don't know of any secrets, youngin'," Tray began. "But one thing is fo' sho'; you must keep waking up, and *that's* everybody's secret!"

"Amen," Dip said, then started walking toward the club. Tray grabbed his arm.

"What's up?" Dip questioned.

"Let's talk out here," came the reply. "I haven't been here in a minute, and security has always been top priority. I can't vouch for what's in there now, but we're safe out here."

"Okay, that's understandable. Besides, who can argue with the teacher?"

Tray smiled, then slapped Dip on the back. "That's right, Daniel, son," Tray joked, as they broke out in laughter.

"Seriously," Tray emphasized, "this Julio situation can get really fucked up really fast for a lot of people."

"Shit, who you telling?" Dip countered. "The way I see it, he'll need an act of Congress before he'll be able to hit the streets again. You know him better than me, Tray. Is he built for what he's facing?"

"Don't know, Dip. I can't speak for his heart or his loyalty. Who knows where they may lie in times of conflicts and challenges."

"What you suggesting?"

"We must touch him — and fast. No hesitation," Tray responded.

"This is Julio we're talking about," Dip insisted.

"Fuck him. He had a choice. It backfired! The stupid muthafucka could've gotten out of this rat race. He took another route, plain and simple. The government will break him. He's never been faced with the reality of not getting out. We're talking the type of pressure that breaks the hardest of killers. He's no killer, nor is he hard. He's most likely shaking like a bad pair of dice!"

"So, how do we touch him?" Dip inquired.

"That's why I'm down here. I have someone who still works in administration over in Jefferson Parish prison. Now, all we need to do is plant someone around him," Tray insisted.

"What about them Taliban muthafuckas?"

"Bingo! I think that just might work. Then, we'll know for sure the business would be handled fast and efficiently," Tray assured.

"Let's do it then because too much is at stake for us to have loose ends!"

"I'm on that," Tray began. "I'll stop over by the hotel, pick up one of them Taliban, then pick up something special for Julio!"

"That's a good look," Dip said.

"So, how's this club thing going for Trim?"

"Sales are down as we anticipated. However, the li'l nigga been booking more shows a week, then he added a kitchen too. He's running it like a sports bar now, day and night. Every Saints game, this place is busting at the scene," Dip boasted.

"Has he taken heed from the jack-ass Julio and dumped that load of shit on another sucka chunking stones at the penitentiary?"

"Don't know for sure, but now is a good time to inquire before we have to engage in the same conversation about him," Dip stated, as they walked toward Trim's club.

Ray-Ray and his death squad were kicked back in one of C-Black's strip clubs, spending big money enjoying themselves while luring for Kane to surface. "There's one sure thing about money," Ray-Ray considered. "It creates new friends." He'd already served a few of the local dealers, so his name before long would be ringing like a doorbell. Ray-Ray understood that a telephone, telegram, and tell-a-nigga was the quickest way to send or receive information. He tossed more money on the stage as the six-foot tall Amazon dancer named Deluxe shook her ass. Careful not to ask too many questions, Ray-Ray let the information trickle in on its own about the ballers of Atlanta.

Ring, ring, ring . . .

"Hello?" Ray-Ray answered.

"This Joe," came the reply.

"Okay, Joe. I'm supposed to know you?"

"You should. I just spent fifteen grand with you."

"Oh yeah! *That* Joe," Ray-Ray remembered. "What's on your mind, playboy?"

"Trying to get in the game again, big brotha."

"You called the right coach then, playa. What's your location?"

"On my way back from Louisiana," Joe admitted.

"What'cha doing down there?"

"Shit, before I met you my usual contact was dry. But I'm straight now, 'cause I'm tripling my money in New Orleans, being shit so dry. Glad you came around when you did, 'cause this big nigga with dreads came out of nowhere buying up everything. My other line wouldn't sell me shit since this nigga came through throwing money around like he was Escobar!"

Ray-Ray swiftly eased away from the table, then went outside the club. "The nigga still spending money like that?"

Joe hesitated, cautious not to mess up his good thing.

"My other contact, like I said, don't call me no more 'cause dude want to purchase everything. The tripped out part about it is me and this nigga J-Rock grew up together, but the nigga won't sale me a crumb."

"That sounds like some bitch shit to me," Ray-Ray conveniently suggested, hoping to gain information by agreeing with Joe and catering to the disloyalty ultimately showed to him. "Yeah, pimpin', although business is business," Ray-Ray continued. "Real niggas don't turn their backs on family, or definitely not niggas they grew up with. That's some foul shit considering the money you spent that put him in the position to be somebody. Now, yo' money ain't no good no mo'? Who this other nigga is anyway?" Ray-Ray asked as if he were concerned about helping Joe get to the bottom of this foul shit that went down.

"That bitch-ass nigga name is Kane, homie," Joe informed him.

Bingo! "Look, I'ma check into this nigga, 'cause I'm the only nigga I know that's buying dope like that on the street," Ray-Ray assured him. "And that name don't ring a bell in my mind," he lied. "And I know the niggas from the Northern to the Southern Hemisphere with money stacked to the muthafuckin' sky! Like I said, he don't ring no bell. And you say this nigga buy all the dope a nigga can produce?"

"That's what J-Rock told me. And he not a broke nigga by any stretch of the imagination," Joe replied.

"I'd like for that nigga Kane to try to buy me out," Ray-Ray laughed. "I bet he won't try that shit no mo'. My connect goes all the fuckin' way to the jungles of Saigon, like Denzel Washington did in *American Gangsta*. Remember that?"

"Yeah, fool, you can't do nothing but respect that nigga's mind."

"Anyway, fool, if you want me to shut that nigga down with all that 'he could buy anything' talk, set it up," Ray-Ray challenged. "I'll even throw in a little something for you if that nigga is who he say he is, which I doubt. But on the business tip, how much you trying to spend?"

"A half like the last time," Joe boasted.

"Tell you what, nigga. I'ma give you a whole thang so that you can get off that half shit. 'Cause I ain't down with bustin' bags open. I'm really supposed to be fuckin' with major players needing fifty or a hundred of them thangs. Peep this, though. I'm not going to be playing myself for no pocket change, risking freedom and all that good shit, and you shouldn't either. So, every time you score, it's supposed to be for more than the last time or you bullshitin' in the game, and need to get out before something bad happens to you," Ray-Ray explained.

"You right, big homie," Joe said, happy to be getting fronted a half brick, plus discovering a new connect that a nigga could only dream of . . . or so he thought.

"I'm over here at the strip club on the boulevard — the same place as the last time. Don't have me waiting, youngin', 'cause time is money," Ray-Ray insisted.

"I'm pushing it like Rick Ross, yo," Joe shot back, then hung up, increasing his speed on the highway leading him back to Atlanta.

Ray-Ray then dialed his stripper friend from C-Black's other club.

"Hello?" China answered.

"What's happening, sweetie?"

"Oh, what do I owe the pleasure of this call?"

"I miss you!"

"Yeah, right," China shot back. "What do you want, Ray-Ray?" she asked.

"Okay, look. I'm still coolin' out in Hotlanta, but got a local nigga credentials I need to run by you."

"Okay, shoot."

"This nigga named J-Rock. You know him?"

"Yeah, I know him. He cool. Be in the clubs a lot."

"You good with the nigga?"

"I'm good with everybody, baby. All my enemies dead, at least the ones I know of," she said, giggling.

"How about this new nigga he been getting busy with lately?" Ray-Ray asked, just to see how informed she was.

"What he look like, baby?"

"Big nigga with dreads," Ray-Ray replied.

"Yeah, I do see dude at the club on the regular basis with C-Black."

"Look, I got fifty grand that says you can't get him into bed and out of his comfort zone until I get there," Ray-Ray challenged.

"Nigga, you *had* fifty grand," China assured him. "A bitch like me ain't never had a problem with getting a piece of dick of my choosing, and this nigga won't break my streak, either. Let me make some calls; then I'll get back with you, sweetie."

"A'ight, baby, just don't let the next bitch beat you to the bank, ya hear me?"

"Boy, you niggas from New Orleans is some grimy muthafuckas. Where they grow you niggas?"

"Right next to you conniving, money-hungry hoes," Ray-Ray reminded her as they both laughed, then hung up.

Donovan Silva jumped on a flight to New Orleans after hearing of Saul Deblanco's plan to assassinate his children. He leaving seemed like the fatherly thing to do. Call it parental instincts, he acknowledged.

He didn't know what he'd do once he made it. But seeing the city again didn't seem like a bad idea anymore. He read every magazine available on the plane, and they all featured James Johnson. Those kids really knew how to make a father proud. He smiled and thought about what he would say to them once they met, *if* they met. He thought about Tray, his life-long friend. Would Tray remember . . . or even forgive him? Was Tray still alive, or was he still living in New Orleans? Were there any grandkids? Would he be accepted?

The questions steadily flowed through his mind like water from a faucet that would not shut off. He now sat in a rental car parked in front of the home that was his for many years. The same house he married the only woman he ever loved. His kids were all born in this same house, and it represented the happiest days of his life.

Tap, tap, tap.

Donovan was awakened from his daydream as a little boy no more than fifteen stood tapping on the driver's-side window of the rental car. Donovan let the window down.

"Who you lookin' for, mister?"

"No one, to tell you the truth," Donovan replied as he shut the vehicle off and stepped outside. "Aren't you supposed to be in school?"

"Naah, dat's for chumps. I'm grindin'."

"Grindin', huh? What's your name?"

"Li'l Wayne."

"I'm Donovan, Li'l Wayne."

"Dat's what's up," Li'l Wayne said, smiling, then held his fist out for a pound. "You don't look like the police. Are you?"

"Naah, that's for chumps," Donovan insisted, smiling at the young man that reminded him of himself. He then walked over to the house that he used to call home and took a seat on the steps. Li'l Wayne sat next to him. "Where do you live?"

"Right ova' there." The boy pointed to the white, ragged house.

"How long you been staying there?"

"All my life," Li'l Wayne responded.

"Who do you live with?"

"Man, you sho' ask a lot of questions. You sho' you ain't the po-po?" Li'l Wayne questioned, getting ready to jump some fences with the ounce of crack and fifty Ecstasy pills on him.

"Nope, I'm just making sure you're not one," Donovan replied.

"Man, I'm too young to be police."

"I don't know that. You only told me you're not one. You may be one of those junior police or some shit like that, feel me?"

Li'l Wayne pulled out his stash, then showed it to Donavan. "Do dis look like what a police carry around?"

"You got a point, Li'l Wayne. I guess we cool then," Donovan admitted.

"Wha'cha doin' 'round here?"

"I used to live here."

"Dat musta' been a long time ago, 'cause Mr. Johnny been here since Ms. Bertha died," Li'l Wayne stated.

"Yeah, it's been a long, long time ago, but I still call this place home, even though I live in California," Donovan confessed.

"You visitin' someone?"

"Maybe, maybe not. It depends."

"On what?"

"On a lot of things. You want to help me?"

"So, we friends?" Li'l Wayne questioned.

"Maybe. Maybe not."

"Then maybe I'll help you."

"Maybe there's something in it for you," Donovan said as a deal breaker.

"Well, since you put it like that, maybe we got a deal."

"I thought you'd see it my way. Now, all you have to do is put your stash away," Donovan insisted.

Li'l Wayne looked around, then went into his waistband and pulled out a nickel-plated .45 automatic.

"So, I guess we won't be needing this either, huh?"

"Especially not that," Donovan assured him. "You have any more of them surprises on you?"

"Only what'cha seen," Li'l Wayne joked.

"Let's keep it that way for a while. You can go stash that."

Li'l Wayne got up, looked both ways across the street, then dashed out in a mad sprint into his backyard. Donovan noticed there was an unusual amount of traffic to be in a residential area. Also, about a mile down the street, cars were parked alongside the road. Li'l Wayne suddenly dashed back across the street.

"Where we headed?"

"What's down there?" Donovan asked.

"Oh, that's one of them schools for the new cars being built. That one down there is named after Ms. Bertha, who used to stay in this house like you. Her son, James, always used to come through and talk to us. But he got shot up they say on the news."

"Let's go down there and see what's going on; then we're going to Canal Street for a little while," Donovan said.

"You treating?"

"Maybe."

"Man, you drive a hard bargain. So, what's my job anyway?"

"You're my tour guide."

"Why you need one of them? Ain't you from New Orleans?"

"Because I've been gone over fifteen years, and I was taught by a very wise man never to enter a place you don't know how to exit. Had you not appeared to be someone that knew his way around, I would've never let my window down. You were what I needed at the time. So that makes you an omen. Hopefully, a *good* one," Donovan concluded. They then walked toward Ms. Bertha Johnson's School of Technology.

Chapter 18

"Good evening, ladies and gentlemen. I'm your host for the debate forum, Doctor Blunt. I'm joined here today by a few of our local officials and special guests. The chief of police for the city of New Orleans, Chief Ryan, Health and Human Resources director, Ms. Deborah Myers, and a spokesman from Johnson Industries, Mr. Robert Victor."

The audience let out a thunderous applause.

"Thank you, ladies and gentlemen, for joining us as we attempt to debate the pros and cons of the effects this city has embodied since Mr. James Johnson announced his startling discoveries. Let's start with Chief Ryan."

"Chief Ryan, have you seen any changes in crime, good or bad, in these three months?"

"Well, Dr. Blunt, there is absolutely nothing good about crime, first of all. But I'd rather be investigating a car theft instead of a drug-related murder. Nevertheless, there has been a significant drop in the arrest of drug dealers, as well as the crimes related to their activities, such as shootings and murders," Chief Ryan concluded.

"So, would you contribute that decline to drugs being hard to come by since Mr. Johnson's effort to cut off the flow from the foreign countries that supply them?"

"Most definitely! We can trace those declines to the fact of criminals not possessing the ingredients present to ignite all the negative effects associated with drugs being readily accessible," Chief Ryan pointed out. "But there also has been a spike in other areas like burglary, robbery, theft, and domestic violence."

"So, Mr. Victor, can you explain to our viewers, while Johnson Industries envisioned a safe and drug-free society, if your company anticipated a spike in other crimes?"

"Good question. The answer is yes. As we all know, ladies and gentlemen, there's no magic pill to make all our problems go away. A headache, maybe. But not anything close to this magnitude. We can look at the impact in two ways. From the inside out or the outside looking in." He paused for emphasis.

"Now, if you stand in both positions, you'll see many different points of view. But we'll only agree on one, and that one view is that this technology is good for everyone. However, people are standing on the outside doing nothing and still will gripe about the expected changes not happening fast enough.

"True. Crime in those areas is rising. But there must be changes in others to get changes in the worst crimes. It's called cause and effect. This process is like weaning America off drugs, and in one way or another, America depends on it.

"But don't think these people on the outside are going to go away easily. This is what they're good at. Criticizing, and most are being paid to.

"You see, Mr. James Johnson has demonstrated what America could've done years ago with the drug epidemic if the concern ever existed. This is why we call those people the 'outsiders looking in.' They will never see it as the people on the inside because that's where the real work is being done!

"We're not interested in profits at Johnson Industries. We're interested in people. The spike in crime is because of what we've implemented. But do understand that drug dealers and addicts still have to survive and are prepared to do what's necessary for doing just that—by any means available. If they had gotten degrees, there would be no spike, but they didn't.

"Keep in mind, Johnson Industries has done more today than your government ever has to affect change in poverty-stricken communities all over the world. This technology is being taught first to those men and women in the society that usually get the opportunities last. Johnson Industries is paying for their education, and they won't owe us a dime. America has always started the poor off in debt, making them even poorer, then expecting great things. That's not a break, that's quicksand! We're reducing crime in all major areas because we're launching a campaign to get the dealers off the streets and into our schools. We're also bringing this opportunity to the prisons, so these men and women in need of a break in life will get that break; our treat! That's what it looks like from the inside of Johnson Industries," Robert concluded.

"Thank you, Mr. Victor, and all those ideas sound great. I'm sure they'll be solid contributions for the future."

"Ms. Deborah Myers, have you witnessed any

change, good or bad, in your area at Health and Human Resources?"

"Basically, we've seen both. But the thing is that more young women have been trickling into our offices that want to enroll in your schools, but have kids, and they're in need of child care. Unfortunately, the vast amount are on government assistance, and so much red tape exists with the child-care system. Much of the issue is the amount being allocated for child care versus what board-certified programs are charging these days. And that, my friend, is making it impossible for already struggling families to find affordable child care. Second, the demand for child-care services is tripling, and the rogue child care providers are raising rates because of the demand."

"So," Doctor Blunt began, "with the issue of rising child-care costs, can your office contact your constituents in Washington to somehow accommodate the families?"

"That's a negative, Doctor Blunt. We've been given a budget, and it only allots specific amounts per family, per child in the form of vouchers. Simply put, it would take an act of Congress to do something in line with that."

"Ms. Myers, if you were on the inside looking out, as Mr. Victor put it, what would be some things on your to-do list?"

"I think from Johnson Industries' perspective, they're doing exactly what needs to be done. Although I hate to be in a position to please the world, in my opinion, they're very close to doing just that. But my point of emphasis would continue to be on family structure. The earlier a boy learns what a man's role is to his family, the earlier he'll make the transition, then relishes the role. Drugs wouldn't fit into the equation as it has, nor would it be brought into it once that boy becomes a man under a strong family structure. Equally so, a young girl being taught how to become a respectable lady relishes her role within the household. Child care is largely a part of this equation. Quality child care is paramount to our children's learning process also. So what's being taught can't be diluted to the extent of it not conforming to the level of education being offered to more privileged children. This, in essence, creates an already uneven playing field for the not-so-privileged children, and that's an early problem that must be corrected," Mrs. Myers concluded.

"My, my, ladies and gentlemen, we're about out of time. But I would like to thank our guests for taking the time out of their busy schedules to speak on the accomplishments and concerns about our community through positive dialogue that's conducive to our goals, expectations, and views shared by Johnson Industries and our distinguished guests. Today, we collectively took a step forward in learning more about what's being done and what needs to be done. We've also acknowledged that a free and critical mind seeks truth without chauvinism or shame and to seek a better life through knowledge, patience, perseverance, and prayer. We thank you for tuning into WXOK, your number one news station with your up-to-date political, economic, and social information leaders in the African American community. It's been my pleasure to be your host. Dr. H. Blunt, signing off to all our viewers. Peace!"

"Hello, everybody out there tuned into Q104, out here in Hotlanta. I'm Sweet Tee, ya girl giving you the best of both worlds in R&B and Hip-Hop.

"Today, I'm broadcasting live outside of my girl, Diamond Monroe's, recently opened hair care store located on the boulevard, 'Diamonds and Girls.' There are five locations spread out over Atlanta, and I ain't mad at cha' for these ridiculously low prices. But I know others are. So without further delay, I'll let her enlighten you on the grand opening of her stores."

"That's right, Atlanta. Diamonds and Girls is definitely in it to win it, as Sweet Tee assured you. Our prices are the lowest in town, and I guarantee it! You heard right, and you can take it to the bank; it's good. Today, for my grand opening, we have free food and drinks all day to show my appreciation for your support. I'm here in the ATL to put the game on lock and the rest of them people out of business with them ridiculous prices. You know who I'm talking about, so let's keep it hood, and y'all get on out here where it's all good. Diamonds and Girls is the answer, without question," Diamond stated.

"Oooh, wee, girl. You rock that funky joint, and some people gon' be mad at cha'. But I respect yo' gangsta, 'cause everything over here is on point, or Sweet Tea would not be endorsing it. You heard it. It's lie down and stay down for the competition, and it sounds like she meant that! So, y'all get on out here for some fun and major discounts, and tell them I sent you, the hottest of the hot, Sweet Tee of Q104 in Hotlanta."

Diamond and Sweet Tee did a high five after the broadcast. Sweet Tee laid her mic down, then grabbed her Diet Coke resting in a nearby ice cooler. The store front was the only one in the strip mall that stood out thanks to the huge sign with lights and sparkling silver glitter that spelled out Diamond's and Girls.

The day was pleasant under the large tent where Sweet Tee was broadcasting. Customers, onlookers, window-shoppers, and freeloaders alike enjoyed the festivities.

"Didn't I tell you broadcasting was going to be easy?" Sweet Tee asked.

"Girl, you been doing this shit for years. You should be a pro by now."

"You have a nice crowd out there. They like your flow."

"For free food, our people will cross a couple of state lines," Diamond shot back. They fell out laughing.

"Diamond, how in the hell are you able to sell your products so cheap and still turn a profit?"

"It's called homework."

"Them damn Koreans gonna be pissed at you."

"Oh well, it's always better to be pissed off than pissed on, right?"

"Right," Sweet Tee laughed, "but didn't you take some of their employees too?"

"That wasn't my fault. They should've been treating them right. How else was I going to get the information I needed?"

"Girl, you is crazy, just like them New Orleans boys."

"Just trying to make the best of a good situation. Because the myths about hiding information in books is a dead issue, being I bought them Koreans' catalog and contact information from their employees," Diamond smirked.

"Speaking of which, I got something for you." Sweet Tee handed Diamond a copy of Sista Souljah's book, *The Coldest Winter Ever.*

"Girl, I heard this book was good; just never got a chance to read it," Diamond said.

"Well, it's definitely a very good book and with an even better lesson in it," Sweet Tee encouraged, knowing Diamond had all her peas in the pot with Kane, who was in a game that resembled quicksand.

"Girl, this shouldn't take me but a few hours to read. I'ma readologist!"

"Let me guess," said Sweet Tee. "You must read a lot, 'cause that's definitely not a word, girl, with your crazy self! Where's that damn man of yours anyway?"

"Probably in the store counting money. That's his hobby and not a bad one," Diamond stated. "Shit, while he's doing that, I'm going to be in that plush office, relaxing with this book, 'cause my feet are killing me."

"You know where to find me. My equipment people are still doing their thang, flirting with these hoochies, so I'll be out here on air doing the rest of these commercials until about 4:00 p.m.," Sweet Tee said.

"Give me a call if you need me," Diamond suggested, then strolled into the store, where Kane was chilling behind the counter enjoying the sight of how fast the money was pouring in. He saw Diamond and immediately began smiling. He walked over, then gave her a bear hug.

"I heard you on the radio doing your thing," he expressed.

"How did I do?"

"You're a natural, baby."

"I have a good teacher," Diamond confessed.

"Nope, it was your idea, baby. All the credit is yours. I just never doubted you."

"You hanging around here all day?"

"Nope, I'm about to move out. There's some business that needs tending to," Kane admitted.

"I'm expecting you home early tonight. I have something special planned."

"In that case, I'll make it an early day," Kane promised, then slapped Diamond on the butt.

"Ouch, boy. I'ma get you back. Respect it when it comes too."

"Yeah, yeah, you'll get your chance, but for now, that ass is mines, and I reserve the right to spank it anytime I want to."

"Okay, Mr. Man, just don't be late," Diamond reminded him, then gave him a big hug and a kiss.

Kane turned, exited the store, then walked through the massive place that used to be a warehouse. En route to her office to unwind, Diamond cracked open the book in her hand as she entered the office, kicked off her shoes, and reclined on the comfortable sofa, then started reading.

The book was very good as Sweet Tee had said it would be. Diamond had been reading for over two hours and only got up to retrieve bottled water out of the fridge. She was almost finished when she received a call from her cousin Carla in New Orleans. She hadn't heard from Carla in months. "I wonder what's wrong," she said aloud.

"Hey, girl. What your tired ass doing?" Diamond joked.

"Look who's talking, Ms. Don't Let A Bitch Know If She All Right!"

"Girl, stop all that sentimental shit. I know my gangsta-ass auntie taught you better than that."

"I'm just concerned about you, girl. You know we were as thick as thieves, and then you just up and leave me," Carla shot back.

"I know," Diamond replied, "but desperate times call for desperate measures, feel me?"

"Yeah, I feel you," Carla said.

"Now, what else is wrong?" Diamond demanded to know.

Carla hesitated for a moment, only because she knew this news would hurt her cousin.

"Where you at?" Carla asked.

"In my office, why?"

"Your office? What, you have a new job?"

"No, baby. I opened five hair care stores today."

"Girl, stop lying!" Carla said.

"No, I'm not, girl. It's real, and I wish you were here with me."

"Let's talk about that later. What's goin' on down there? Are you by yourself right now?" Carla questioned.

"Yeah, I'm alone. What's up?"

"Look, a bitch name Tara down here always coming through Keoka's boutique, talkin' about she's carrying Kane baby."

"Say what!" Diamond shouted.

"Yeah, Dee, me, and her had never met, but Keoka had been lacing me up with the info; then fate would have it we meet up one day at the boutique. She running her mouth."

Diamond's heart was pounding as she listened to the disturbing news. She was now praying it wasn't true. But she knew Kane was a street nigga, and anything was possible.

"So what happened next?"

"I just continued shopping and listening to all the things she said her and Kane used to do as she started pulling out pictures. After that, I lost it, girl. 'Cause all she talked about was Kane and me this, Kane and me that. So I asked her since they were so close, then why he leave her behind? The bitch came back hard on my ass, girl."

"What she say?"

"The bitch said Kane left her what she needed . . . money!"

Diamond's mind was again scheming at a frantic pace.

"Oooh, girl," Carla continued, "I was heated in that store, then she said something that made me forget she was pregnant. It was some real shit, but I wasn't functioning from a real state of mind."

"Uh-huh."

"The bitch said let the next ho take the chances, and that she was the smart bitch in his crew of bitches."

"So, you think the bitch telling the truth?" Diamond asked.

"That's why I ran on her ass. All that shit sounded authentic, but I wasn't going to let her get away with calling you a ho either."

Diamond was now thinking about what Winter's mother went through with Santiaga in Sista Souljah's book and vowed not to let the same thing happen to her.

"Hellooo, are you still there?" Carla inquired.

"Yeah, girl, I'm still here. Just figuring out my next move. This nigga taught me well. Maybe too well," Diamond admitted. "Look, I'ma take a trip out there just to look around. But I want you to come back up here to live with me. You game?"

"You know I am. We're sisters for life, girl."

"I need you to get that bitch address. I'll be there in about a week. It's going down," Diamond promised, now standing up in the middle of her office, getting ready to go home and prepare a special night for Kane.

"That won't be a problem, Dee. Her credit card information should reveal that. I'll get it from Keoka."

"Tell my auntie I'm coming to see her next week and not to tell anyone," Diamond insisted.

"Consider it done, cuz. Anything else?" Carla asked.

"Yeah, go by Barnes & Nobles, then pick up Sista

Souljah's book, *The Coldest Winter Ever.* Read it; then you'll understand my next move."

"What the fuck, you a teacher now?"

"Not exactly. But I learned a very valuable lesson today, and I hope you will too."

"So what was the lesson?" Carla inquired.

"You're never too old to learn, or too smart to do dumb shit," Diamond admitted.

Chapter 19

Luqman's plane landed at the private strip in Houma, Louisiana, not too far from the Fortress. The Fortress had taken six months to build. It was lavishly decorated. He had been in Cuba overseeing the factories, holding board meetings that provided more structure within the troubled country, and negotiating with workers. Things had gotten back to normal, yet a few militant groups wanted in on the drug profits from the trade. Regrettably, they wanted war at a time when peace was on the table, so Johnson Industries refused to purchase their drugs. To defuse the situation, a vicious assault was launched against the militants for an entire week. When it was over, not a militant was left to tell the story of the devastation that had occurred.

Now back in the States, Luqman had a very busy schedule ahead of him, especially with the Julio situation looming. Troy and Maria were en route from Colombia, and Jaafar from the mountains of Afghanistan. They all agreed things could get real messy, real fast. There weren't many options on the table. The most popular was that Julio had to be terminated.

Luqman dialed Tray.

"Hello?" Tray answered.

"I've made it. Where do you want to meet?"

"The Fortress," came the reply.

"I'm a few minutes away. See you then."

Ring, ring, ring . . .

"Hello," Deon answered.

"This Luqman. You busy?"

"Not for you. What's up?"

"Can you and Dip meet me at the Fortress?"

"We'll be there shortly. How was your trip?"

"It was very busy over there in Cuba."

"I can hear the truth of that statement in your voice."

"Hey, where's Troy and Maria?"

"They should be landing along with Jaafar any minute. They'll be at the Fortress too," Luqman assured her.

"I'll see you in a few then. Let me locate Dip," Deon said as she hung up shortly afterward.

"Crossroads Rehabilitation Center, may I help you?"

"Yes, ma'am. Could you please connect me to room 617?" the caller asked.

"Just one minute, sir."

"Hello," Joy answered.

"Yes, I'd like to speak to Mr. Johnson. It's of a rather important nature," Hector Satorie stated.

"May I ask how you learned of Mr. Johnson's whereabouts?"

"That's a very good question, Ms. Whoever-You-Are. But the most important concern is not that I know; it's someone who's an enemy of his knowing. So we can play cat-and-mouse games all you want, or you can allow me to save his life possibly," Hector stated.

"One minute," Joy said, handing James the phone.

"Put it on intercom," James demanded, curiously eyeing Salvator seated across from him.

"James speaking."

"Yes, Mr. Johnson. It's good to hear you're doing well. But I must inform you that your location has been compromised."

"And how would you know this?"

"Because I'm able to reach you quicker than I can Pizza Hut," Hector replied.

"Who are you, and why are you so concerned?" James shot back.

"My name is Hector Satorie, and I represent a portion of California under the Cali Cartel, controlled by Saul Deblanco."

James eyed Salvator. Salvator nodded, indicating he knew of him.

"As for why I'm concerned, let's just say I think I'm picking a winner in this race. This war Saul has decided to wage against you is done without my support. Saul has acquired your location and has a team of assassins headed your way as we speak. You should immediately vacate the facility you are presently occupying," Hector seriously stated.

James sat there a minute in deep thought, massaging his temples.

"Where can I find Saul?" James asked, ready to speed up his plans to assassinate everyone that comes up against him.

"He's presently in California. I can get you his daily

whereabouts, but for now, you and your people don't have much time to debate about leaving. You should be gone. From my understanding, all hell will be unleashed very quickly. James, you have an ally in me. I'll be in touch, or Salvator knows how to reach me. God bless." The line went dead.

"James," Joy said, jolting him out of his trance, then handing him the cell phone, "it's Irvin."

"What's up, Irvin?"

"Look, I have General McCloud and a team coming to get all of you. Your location is about to be raided. We just intercepted information that Saul Deblanco has sent men to make another attempt on your life. He also has men on the ground in New Orleans. But first things first. The general is flying in there. The road leaving out is too dangerous. These men are rumored to possess tons of explosives, and there's a good chance they'll detonate the entire facility," Irvin advised.

"This place is like a damn fortress," James reminded him.

"So was your mansion in Slidell. Yet, as I now recall, it's a vacant lot. Am I correct?" Silence crept across the phone lines. "As I stated, James, I need for all of you to start making your way toward the back of the facility. Whenever Saul's men arrive, it'll be through the front entrance, and you'll hear them before you see them. The general will land the Tomahawk in the safest and farthest place from the entrance. I've alerted all local authorities. I'm guessing by the time they make it, you'll all be gone and the assassination team trapped. The general will call once he lands, so you should be out of the doors *now*," Irvin insisted.

James mentally gathered himself, then hung up the phone.

"Let's go, everyone. Seems Hector was right about Saul's men en route. Irvin intercepted information that the assassins are due here any minute. He also confirms them cocksuckers will be loaded down with explosives, so we'll hear them before we see them. General McCloud will set the Tomahawk down in the back of the facility," he concluded.

"Please tell me the explosive information was only a joke," Joy pleaded.

"It's real, baby — no joke. But we only need to make it to the back of the facility before they get here," James said.

"Well, baby. Let's go," she responded. "I've heard and experienced enough explosives to last a lifetime. How far do we have to go?"

"There are three buildings with checkpoints to go through if we want to bypass going outside and eliminating the chances of being noticed," Salvator replied.

"Damn, we don't have any weapons!" James angrily stated, kicking the chair across the room.

"Oh no, my friend. You're wrong. We have *many* weapons," Salvator assured him.

"How'd you pull that off?" Joy inquired, as Salvator opened the closet door, revealing a green army duffel bag full of guns, grenades, and ammunition.

"All of them pretty nurses you wanted me to leave

alone, they wanted me to leave here in good condition and made sure to get me exactly what I needed to make that possible," Salvator said. He grabbed the bag, then peeped out the door in both directions. Everything was quiet as the nurses continued about their business, attending to their patients, not knowing the drama that was about to unfold any minute. But the only person who would notice them with the bag would be the ugly receptionist that was hired a week ago and seemed always to monitor their movements, Salvator suspected.

"Look, guys," Salvator began, "even my charm won't help us with this new, ugly receptionist. If she sees all of us leaving at one time, she may get suspicious, then try to get in the way of us catching our flight on time. I have a plan. I'm going to stroll past her while the two of you make a run for the back of the facility as fast as you can. Here, take these vests. There's something not right, and I never ignore my instincts. Take these guns, James. Here, Joy, a little one for you, so don't hurt yourself — or us. You do know how to use one, right?"

"Probably not to your standards, but point and shoot, correct?"

"Exactly, but aim for his dick, so if you miss, his chest will surely suffer from your mistake," Salvator laughed.

He then reached into the bag and pulled out a nine-inch Rambo knife inserted into its sheath located in his waistband.

"I think this ugly duckling has been in our business long enough. It's going to be her fucking birthday today, my friends," Salvator promised.

"Don't worry. I won't make the scene. She won't even though she's dead until she sees that white light people speak of when they die and come back. But she won't be coming back from the light. Look, I'm leaving first. Then you two, five seconds after me, head in the opposite direction. If I'm not in that helicopter five minutes after the explosions begin . . . leave," Salvator demanded.

"Damn, man, you must enjoy being left behind," James said. "Why don't we all just get the hell out of here right now?"

"Then how will we know if we're being followed if we're just running? What if we run out of this room, then the ugly person sitting behind that desk calls ahead to her buddies who ambush us? No, my friends. I will start with her, and if anyone is following you, I will be following them, and you know I won't miss them for all the blood diamonds in Africa," Salvator assured him.

James thought long and hard about what his friend was saying and knew Salvator had done his homework. He thought about what Joy had called him, Mr. Behind-Enemy-Lines. That's when he was at his best, when others would be at their weakest. What made him the best is that he always volunteered for the job nobody else wanted. He stood behind enemy lines so that the rest of the team would be safe . . . the ultimate sacrifice . . . the ultimate warrior.

"Right," James told him. "I know you won't miss them."

"Then stop talking and start counting to five once I leave this room," Salvator demanded.

He then left with nothing but the knife tucked into his waist. Salvator walked past the receptionist slowly, and when her attention was diverted by Joy and James leaving the room, he dipped. When she turned around, Salvator was nowhere in sight. The ugly woman reached for the phone, then suddenly froze in midair. She dropped the phone as her entire body went dead. Her mind was still able to wonder about what had happened, but she couldn't feel her arms or legs. She was paralyzed but didn't know why. Salvator kneeled in a crouched position behind the receptionist with the Rambo knife plunged into her spinal cord. Her eyes darted back and forth as she caught a glimpse of the man the world had known as the "Whisper." Salvator held a finger to his lips as he indicated to the woman that it was all over. He then pulled the knife out of her, then plunged it into the left side of her back, slicing open her heart. When she fell to the floor, her eyes were wide open, as if she'd just smoked some crack. But Salvator was gone before the body hit the floor, as if he were a ghost.

James and Joy continued at a steady pace, traveling outside the facility, rather than chance being caught inside. Suddenly, all hell broke loose behind them. The explosion seemed a long way out but still shook the ground. Security was running around, barking orders for everyone to get back inside. The two ignored the orders, taking their chances outside, as they now heard something that resembled a helicopter. Another explosion rocked the building they recently passed.

"How the hell did that happen?" James questioned.

"What?" Joy inquired.

"I know the first explosion had to be the front entrance, but how'd the next explosion get so close so fast?"

"Shit!" Joy stated. "They must have people here setting explosives too. But who?"

James slid the Glock into his right hand, then reached and retrieved the other Glock with his left.

"Let's go!" he said, as he began trotting.

"How far do we have to go?" Joy asked.

"About a hundred yards or so."

Suddenly, the sounds of automatic gunfire were heard not too far away . . . followed by the sound of an explosion.

"That was close," Joy stated with the sound of panic in her voice, still running.

"That was a grenade. Salvator must be right behind us. Hurry!"

Suddenly the Tomahawk could be seen descending into an open space in the back of the last building. Five men exited the helicopter and surrounded the machine with high-powered artillery.

General McCloud was seen waving from the helicopter at James and Joy to hurry, as more explosions grew near. Out of nowhere, Salvator appeared with a rocket launcher, running toward the Tomahawk. When he was about fifty yards away, he turned around and kneeled on one knee, then fired the rocket into a vehicle full of men chasing him. He then tossed the launcher off his shoulder, running as fast as he could, zigzagging his way toward the helicopter as more gunfire was exchanged.

General McCloud ran back to the controls, strapped himself in, and was waiting on his last passenger. James kneeled in a crouched position from within the helicopter, firing away at the men on foot chasing Salvator as he dove into the helicopter.

"Go! Go! Go!" James yelled as he continued to let off rounds, dropping several more assassins.

The helicopter lifted instantly as the soldiers continued launching a brutal attack on the assassins within the range with the Gatling gun on board.

"We must stop meeting like this!" General McCloud yelled at Salvator's back.

"Not as long as I'm with him!" Salvator yelled back, pointing at James as they all joined in on the joke, laughing.

As the helicopter breezed through the air, Salvator put his arm around James's neck, and at that time, the two men truly understood how much they meant to each other.

"Where we headed?" Joy asked in a loud voice, barely able to hear herself over the massive machine.

"There's a piece of land that I want to show James in Houma!" the general said with a wink.

The information Irvin had prepared for Dip through his technology team had revealed Akbar's exact location. Jaafar had managed to plant a homing device under Akbar's car a month ago when he followed him after a meeting he had set up with his friend, Ahmed, from Baton Rouge. Jaafar had left for Afghanistan, but the homing device provided coordinates for the team of technicians paid to follow and monitor the whereabouts of Akbar for the past thirty days.

The monitors displayed everywhere Akbar had traveled the past month. Dip wanted all the discs. He decided that Akbar would die instead of prospering like he thought he would. Dip had given the green light to kidnap Akbar and the family he now lived with in Baton Rouge.

Akbar was presently at the store, along with Ahmed and his family, when a black van pulled up. Three men casually exited it, then strolled into the store. Minutes later, everyone was facedown on the floor. After searching the store thoroughly, they escorted Akbar and the entire Ahmed family into the van. He knew what time it was, and so did Ahmed. The men locked the doors to the business, then tossed the keys to Ahmed. This was a message to him that they came for only one thing and one person.

Ahmed had a copy of the disc, but would not try to conceal it at the cost of him and his family losing their lives. Everyone was silent the entire ten-minute trip. The van pulled into a garage at a home in Zachary, Louisiana. There were no houses in the area within a two-mile radius in any direction. Everyone was escorted into the modestly furnished home, then the man in charge pulled out his cell phone, dialed, and started speaking into the phone. After a minute, he handed the phone to Akbar.

"Hello?" Akbar answered.

"The rules have changed again," Dip stated with sarcasm.

"I see," Akbar agreed.

"You should have taken the money I offered, my friend."

"So, you blame me for taking advantage of an opportunity of a lifetime?"

"Not really. I probably would have done the same thing."

"So, how about we call it even, then I give you the money Kane gives me?"

"That's a very attractive offer, but no lesson would be learned. Plus, it goes against all I've been taught."

"Who cares about a lesson when there are millions on the table!" Akbar brazenly said, considering his position.

"One who strives for greatness and power. That's something not associated with money or fame. Knowledge is something you can't see, only sense. Yet, it provides the beholder with more in life than any amount of money ever could," Dip stated. "Not to mention, money is why you're in your position, and knowledge is why I'm in my position. So, do you now see the lesson?"

"I understand that my need of money is why I'm in this position."

"No!" Dip spoke in a confident tone. "The *love* of money put you in this position! I gave you an out, and you got greedy. You became an enemy to me when you put my freedom in jeopardy. So my knowledge demands I never leave an enemy behind to rise against me," Dip assured Akbar.

"What choices do I have?" Akbar asked, looking for a way out of the grim reality of his present crisis.

"There are two," Dip suggested, his face now revealing a sinister smile.

"One involves my men escorting you down into a torture chamber and extracting the disc's location slowly and painfully. Or, two, you can hand them over and die quick and quiet."

"What will happen to Ahmed and his family?"

"That's none of your concern. Your decision to involve them and their willingness to assist you may prove fatal to them as well. But we will see."

"They know nothing of what's contained on the disc," Akbar pleaded.

"If so, they have nothing to worry about. Now, please hand the phone to my protégé. There's nothing left for us to discuss."

Akbar did as he was told, then started to apologize to his friend and his family in Arabic. He told them that he would die today, and may Allah bless them not to meet the same fate as he.

The men began escorting Akbar out of the room and into another when suddenly he turned around and stated, "As-salaamu alaikum."

The entire family in unison responded with, "Wa alaikum as-salaam."

Chapter 20

Julio was in his cell doing pushups when the white guy in the day room strolled over to him after watching his daily soap opera.

"The deputy said you have a visitor, homie."

A visit, Julio thought. *Who could this be?* He cut his workout short, grabbed a towel, washed his face, hands, and then started brushing his coal-black hair. The cell door suddenly slid opened, and Julio strolled out into the hallway where he was handcuffed, then escorted to the visiting shed.

As he was leaving, a new guy was being brought into the tier and assigned the vacant cell a few doors down from Julio. The guy looked to be dirt-poor and lived in the mountains, was Julio's best guess, based on his unkempt, long, scraggly gray beard, dirty hands, and worn clothing. He began to wonder again about his visitor. *Who could this possibly be?* His question was answered as the door opened. Agent John Cage of the Federal Bureau of Investigations sat there, awaiting him.

"Long time no see!" John expressed.

"Didn't know we were friends," Julio shot back.

"Don't you want to be? I can make it happen."

"Yeah, right. Man, you're only concerned with your funky-ass investigation. My situation is the last thing on your sympathy list," Julio stated.

"Let's not waste time then. Have you thought about whether you want to see the streets again?"

"Never considered not seeing them again in the equation. Justice hasn't prevailed."

"You should. We have a pretty strong case against you, Julio. There really isn't a legitimate reason for you to be confident."

"Don't believe in miracles, do you?" Julio shot back.

"Not against us, Julio. We go by the book."

"It's not up to you. It's up to those twelve jurors seated in the jury box."

"That's why we go by the book, so there's nothing else to weigh but what we've presented as evidence. You see, we don't come unless we got you. We don't ask questions we don't already have the answers to. And above all, we, under no circumstances, waste taxpayers' time or money."

Julio smiled. "That's a nice speech you have there, John. Top notch! But how many people put their money on Peyton Manning in the Super Bowl, when it should've been on Drew Brees?"

John shrugged. "Wouldn't know that, my friend."

"Exactly," Julio agreed. "That's why they play the game, my friend."

"A lot of people out there are getting nervous since you been in here," John said, changing the subject.

"I didn't know you cared. Who are these people, so I can remind them that they're the ones free? Why would they be nervous?"

"That's what I'm hoping to get from you. Some

names, then all your worries can be over with the stroke of a pen," John promised.

"What makes you think I know anything about anybody you don't even have evidence against? I'll tell you what. You tell me who you're speaking of, and maybe we can get somewhere . . . or maybe not."

"James Johnson ring any bells?"

"You mean the lawyer guy who was almost killed?"

"That's him. You know him personally?" John inquired.

"You're joking, right?"

John's expression remained stoic.

"I guess not," Julio shot back.

"I take it you're denying any affiliation?"

"Man, you're the Feds. What do you think?"

"I guess you can't help me then. It's no sweat off my back. Just a little word of advice for free. Watch yourself in here. All your friends have returned to the States since your arrest. That's very interesting, don't you think?"

Julio shrugged.

"You're pretty cool about this information, but I'd give a king's ransom to know the topic of their conversation," John voiced.

"Look, Agent, you're wasting your precious time here entertaining me. Truth is, I don't know anything about your suspects or their business."

"That's your final answer?"

"That's my word," Julio shot back.

John slid his chair back, then knocked on the locked door for the guard. He glanced back at Julio, then shook his head as if the man were doomed. John exited the visiting area.

The door slid open, and Julio strolled into the tier. He walked toward his cell, looking cautiously at Abu, feeling troubled. Abu walked to his cell gate, as Julio walked past him. He watched Julio as he picked up the telephone on the wall, then began dialing. For some reason, Julio sensed something and turned around to see Abu staring at him.

"Don Hamas, how have you been, my friend?" Don Giodana asked as Don Hamas strolled over to the table located in the back of an Italian restaurant on Don Giodana's turf. Already at the table were Don Santos, Don Cardone, Don Silva, and Don Cardona.

"I've been better, but I've also been worse. Can't complain; nobody listens," Don Hamas said. "It's good to see you survived the hit them blackies put you through."

"Yeah, well, it's just another war story to reminisce about with the grandkids. Them boys won't be making promises they can't keep anymore. You can take *that* to the bank," Don Giodana boasted.

"Very good. What's the hot topic of the day?"

"Look, Don Hamas, there are opinions among the rest of us about James Johnson. None of us anticipated all the drama within the States, and simply put, are feeling as though James is using us to further his agenda," Don Silva suggested.

"Oh, so you men are now having second thoughts about your foolproof plan?" Don Hamas questioned.

"On the contrary. Mr. Johnson has fulfilled all his spoken obligations. It's just different than what we're used to," Don Cardone said.

"That figures. You men are bosses, and you come up under bosses and their bosses," Don Hamas stated. "You're goddamn straight it's different! You all have a boss now, and it's James Johnson! You men have single-handedly disgraced centuries of heritage. Our ancestors must be turning over in their graves to see you sell out traditions as rich and deeply rooted as the Mafia's!"

"Look, we're not here for history lessons, Don Hamas. We're here because our sources report that you're making significant moves, and if so, maybe we want in," Don Giodana stated.

"And what moves might that be, Don Giodana? I'm into many things."

"We hear the Mexican Mafia isn't too thrilled about Mr. Johnson or his current policy either. And we know for sure they assassinate with regularity."

Don Hamas smiled as the Commission expressed its reluctance in being under this black man's control. He was equally surprised at how much they knew about his moves concerning the Mexican Mafia. He wondered if they could've stumbled upon any of his meetings with the CIA agent.

"What exactly are you proposing? There has to be a catch," he said.

"Maybe we want things as they were, simple as that."

"What are you prepared to do to accomplish this goal?"

"Whatever it takes to undo this current situation," Don Cardone insisted.

"What about all the money you received from Mr. Johnson?"

"We were making that money *before* Mr. Johnson's proposition. The only reason we went along with the idea was the threat of drugs becoming obsolete. But if you have opened a drug market through the Mexican Mafia, then we want in. Fuck Mr. Johnson!" Don Cardona expressed.

He glanced around the table at the four dons that made up the Commission. *I wonder if they truly understand what they're agreeing to.* Confident that he had them under his control, Don Hamas continued explaining his strategy.

"So, do I have this entire Commission's approval of my affiliation?"

The four dons glanced at each other, then nodded their approval, which was the first step of an all-out war against James.

"Then it's done," Don Hamas agreed. "Now, I can let you men in on what I've been working on."

Meanwhile, Don Santos had been reluctant to be a part of this decision but resigned to play his part of the game to perfection, as he'd already contacted James with the details of the Commission's change of heart and the location of today's meeting.

Acting on that tip, James dispatched Irvin's security team to bug the entire meeting equipped with audio and video surveillance.

On the other hand, Don Hamas stood pleased at the Commission's unanimous vote. He was secretly wearing a wire that recorded everything. Armed with this critical evidence of betrayal against the Commission, he planned on delivering it to James, and to lead the Commission into a vicious slaughter at the hands of James, for their transgressions against him as proof to James of his loyalty. What the hell, why not propose that there be no Commission again—ever! Don Hamas now figured that he'd proposed all states left by the demise of the late Commission be given to him since it was his plan that sealed their fate.

The don began laying his trap to perfection.

"Gentlemen, I must admit, you've done your homework. There is a pipeline I've established through the Mexican Mafia. The existing president will be assassinated in Mexico. He has interfered with the drug trade induced by James Johnson, and he will die because of it. Quickly, things will be back to normal once that happens," Don Hamas promised. "A new government is already poised to take control immediately. There will exist some brutal wars shortly in Mexico, my friends. But rest assured, drugs will flow through those borders like they once did," Don Hamas said.

"So, what do you think Mr. Johnson will be doing while you're replacing governments?" Don Cardona asked.

"Certainly not standing and watching," Don Santos shot back.

"That's correct. But remember, Mr. Johnson isn't

occupying Mexico because of violence; it's because of government. Mr. Johnson is controlling the drug trade because of his politics, yet violence, not politics, once controlled Mexico. That's the Mexico that creates a free flow of drugs into the United States and abroad. There are thousands of deaths annually in Mexico involving drug wars. What I've merely done is ignited a fire in the right people who'll produce as much death and violence within Mexico's government to assure our drugs flow through those borders like water," Don Hamas reported.

"Then that leaves us with nothing else to discuss but how and when to take down Mr. Johnson's empire," Don Giodana suggested.

"Not so fast, my friend. Choose your enemies wisely in this high-stakes game. How, you ask? Allow me to continue to develop strategies. Our moves will be at precise times, catching our enemies at their weakest. When? Preferably, in turmoil and conflict, which would demand their attention," Don Hamas lobbied.

"I'm curious," Don Santos began. "What makes you an expert on Mr. Johnson?"

"First of all, you called me. Second, either you're too scared to do anything, or you didn't know where to start. Either way, I'm here, because you knew I wasn't going to willingly allow Mr. Johnson free reign to rearrange the Italian culture. That doesn't prove me an expert, but it does prove I still have my balls . . . unlike some others," Don Hamas laughed.

The Commission considered Don Hamas's statement individually, and each knew he hit the nail on the head.

But the fearful questions did arise: What if they failed? What would be the consequences? Would James slaughter their families? Could they trust Don Hamas with power that could put all their lives in jeopardy? What other choices did they have, other than to feel every day as if they were selling out a culture of rich tradition that has been present for centuries? Would they trust an outsider, rather than one of their own? Each don considered these questions.

However, if walls could talk, they'd speak of unthinkable deception from within the same rich tradition that would, no doubt, lead to possibly the destruction of the Mafia as a culture . . . at the hands of one of their very own.

Kane made it home as promised to Diamond. His conversation with J-Rock had produced a supposed major connect with a grade-A product and unlimited quantities. He desperately longed to meet this person as he now thought of the one point five million-dollar wire transfer to Akbar. The streets would pay for his losses in the form of taxes on his product.

Diamond strolled into the room with nothing on but a look that screamed, "Come and get it!"

"Yo, yo, J-Rock. Let me get back at you later. There's something of an emergency that just walked in."

"Okay, big homie. Get at me," J-Rock stated, then hung up.

Diamond seductively strolled past Kane, peeping

back, then motioning with her finger for him to follow. He stood, then began his pursuit as if under a trance. Instinctively, he unbuckled his jeans, leaving them in his tracks, as he did his shirt, shoes, and jewelry.

Diamond continued twisting her sexy, 36-24-36 dynamic, athletic, fit body through the kitchen that led to the Jacuzzi. She'd stocked the small refrigerator on the side of the Jacuzzi with chocolate-covered strawberries, Cool Whip, honey, and a few cigars laced with Purple Haze that would no doubt set the mood right. She then dipped her pretty feet into the Jacuzzi, testing the water temperature. She turned toward Kane, then stated, "Perfect."

She slowly descended into the Jacuzzi enjoying the bubbles generated by the powerful jet streams. She looked back once more at Kane, then bent over so that he could get a good view of her pussy from the back. Kane was trying to open a bottle of Moët, but momentarily abandoned the task and grabbed a 'gar and began watching Diamond as his dick stood at attention like a World War II vet at a funeral.

"I got this, baby. You just get comfortable. It's gonna be a long night."

"I hope so," she said seductively.

She now had her arms spread along the back of the Jacuzzi floating her body to the top, opening and closing her legs.

Kane handed her a glass of Moët as he entered the water with a 'gar ablaze hanging from his lips and another glass in hand.

"We have arrived," Kane toasted. They clinked their glasses, interlocked arms, and sipped the Moët.

Diamond stood and reached below the water for Kane's dick. She stroked it, then turned around and sat on it, making sure every inch was inside of her. She handed him the empty glass and slowly grinded her hips and ass back and forth in his lap.

Kane puffed on the Purp, then reached around and placed the 'gar in between Diamond's lips. As she puffed, she grinded and rode Kane like a cowgirl in a rodeo. Up and down and around and around she went as the soulful sounds of Jaheim flowed in the background, encouraging men to "Put That Woman First."

Kane was feeling like a real don as his eyes were closed, but his mind was wide open, thinking about the bright future ahead of him.

Diamond continued throwing pussy every which way that helped her achieve an orgasm and to make sure Kane received the ride of his life. She turned to look at him, thinking about the fact of him fathering a child with another bitch while she lay in danger of getting her head knocked off. She now remembered reading *The Coldest Winter Ever*, and then decided she would not suffer the same fate. The lesson in Sista Souljah's book was a game changer. She'd be damned if she'd be without or put in prison for the rest of her life, and the outside bitch ends up with everything. *Hell no, not after all my time, blood, sweat, and tears! People who don't take heed to history by any standard are doomed to repeat it,* she thought as she continued to pleasure the man she now saw as a threat and would ultimately make an example of.

Kane aggressively grabbed her by the waist, sliding in and out of her pussy, slapping water everywhere from the sudden pound game he unleashed to show her that he always hits his mark. The vicious onslaught continued as Diamond screamed and moaned, engulfed in total orgasmic chaos. The screams of excitement made Kane go harder, stronger, and longer than usual. There was no doubt in his mind about his dicksman's status as he worked Diamond's pussy overtime. Like a silent assassin, the feeling of a sudden explosion crept up his loins, activating a more serious villain inside his mind that made him grab Diamond, seating her in his lap, then slowly grinding her rough and rugged. He slid all nine and a half thick inches inside her pussy, bouncing short strokes to make sure that the "pain is love" theory resonated in her mind, body, and soul.

"Oooh wee, baby!" Diamond protested as she was in a serious bear hug that had produced back-to-back orgasms and completely exhausted her. Kane's concentration remained as serious as the recession and drought put together. His grasp suddenly increased as he leaned her forward placing one hand on her stomach, then pulled her to him. The other hand was planted in the middle of her back, pushing her pussy up and in plain view, as he stood up on the steps of the Jacuzzi. He went to work like a surgeon on Diamond's clean-shaven pussy. The water was splashing out of the Jacuzzi as if it were being thrown out with a bucket as Kane pumped. Suddenly, his grip released, and his body tensed up as he leaked sperm into Diamond's pussy by the ounce, as she now shivered too. Once he was drained of everything within him, he fell backward into the water with a big splash.

"How was it?" Diamond asked after he resurfaced.

"Like it always is, baby. The best I ever had and ever will," he promised.

The statement activated Diamond's inner demon as she reached into the fridge, retrieving the strawberries and Cool Whip. *If you have the best already, then what do you need another for, if it's not to take her place?* she reasoned within. Then she remembered what Sista Souljah said: "There's no such thing as love any more, the kind that is so strong that you can feel it in your bones!"

Chapter 21

President Malik Quinn was seated in his comfortable chair in the Oval Office at the White House listening to his senior adviser, press secretary, economic adviser, and chief of staff.

"Mr. President, there has to be a way to solve this crisis, and it has to involve Mr. Johnson," his economic director assured him.

"So what are you telling me? Is that because Mr. Johnson has stopped the flow of drugs into the United States, it's hurting our markets?"

"That's part of it. The other is that he has crippled the oil industry, and you know how much our economy depends on that industry."

"So do the Saudis, tycoons, and Texas billionaires!" Malik shot back.

"You're one hundred percent correct, Mr. President. Be that as it may, significant holes still remain that need to be plugged. To add insult to injury, Mr. Johnson's technology replaces no viable investment opportunities, being that his company is one hundred percent owned, operated, and not traded through shares to anyone."

"What's wrong with that? This is still a free country, right?" Malik asked.

"What's wrong with it? He's monopolized the market.

Mr. Johnson's ideas are wreaking havoc on the markets and our economy, Mr. President!"

"So, is that all Mr. Johnson is doing for our economy?"

"I don't understand, sir. Isn't what I just described enough?"

"Hell no, it's not enough!" Malik yelled. "Tell me the whole damn story when you come speaking about an issue. I could give a good goddamn about the rich and their cries about not getting richer. They happen to be worth more than ninety-five percent of America. So what if they're losing money? I'm more concerned about the poor and the middle-class citizens who actually work for a living. It's about damn time they were told no; they can't have some of someone else's cake. Tell me about the reduction in crime and violence, the decrease in drug addiction, the creation of environmentally friendly jobs, foreign and domestic, the free education that Mr. Johnson offers to the poor Americans that'll contribute to future leaders and their right to a bright future just like the wealthy. Did you know the profits Mr. Johnson made are being spent on our programs? Did you know, in his first year, he has been more successful in creating jobs and a better quality of life than the government has in its entire existence? Do you know how he's doing it? No politics, no polls, no kissing ass," Malik assured him. He paused for a second, waiting for a reply. There was none. He smiled an evil grin, then asked, "Is this the man you think is *hurting* our economy? Let me get this right. You want me to tell Mr. Johnson to stop what he's doing, so the rich can get richer, and fuck everybody else?"

The economic team sat stoically like imbeciles, having not researched any of the facts Malik spoke of and really couldn't have cared less. Because in Washington, those facts were last on the priority list. Washington clearly placed more concern on polls that win elections, not people, especially the *poor* people.

"Now, does anybody have any other concerns other than the rich, how much money Mr. Johnson is taking from the rich, the Democratic Party, or poll numbers?" Malik inquired.

The team looked at each other, then the chief of staff began his pitch. "With all due respect, Mr. President, those concerns are our jobs."

"No! Your concern is to provide me with more than a one-sided argument for me to base important decisions about leading this country on!" Malik insisted.

"On the contrary. My concern, Mr. President, is to provide you with information that's relevant to the issues that keep you in office. Mr. Johnson, being a philanthropist, makes him one of many that donate their time and money to worthy causes. More importantly is the fact that his cause doesn't help you. It's a potential political nightmare."

"So, you're suggesting I put political ambitions over people?"

"I'm suggesting you survey the demographics of the people who were largely responsible for electing you."

"Let me guess," Malik began. "The people Mr. Johnson is helping aren't part of the demographics, are they?"

"That's correct, Mr. President."

"So, do you suppose I'd tell Mr. Johnson to start letting drugs flow into the United States, because the rich can't get richer without it, and for him to stop making this new technology, so we can stay dependent on the oil industry, instead of the clean, environmentally friendly fuel that he created with these drugs? Then, if all those demands are met, I would be essentially making him close down all the schools teaching this new technology to the poor and second-class citizens. So, you propose that I say 'shut it down, Mr. Johnson.' Is that right?"

"My job is to bring facts. And, yes, with political ramifications at the foremost, Mr. President," his chief of staff stated.

"Let's not get it twisted. I'm a president for the people, *not* politics," Malik shot back.

"Right. Yet, we stand to lose many seats in the House and the Senate if this economy doesn't loosen up. The Republicans don't have a clue about fixing it. And the nation wants the change we promised them."

"Maybe one's on the way," Malik said. "At any rate, when you men can come up with solutions rather than complaints, you know where to find me. Until then, I have business to attend to."

The men slowly filed out of the office, not knowing of anything more to do or say to the president, who stood to lose the presidency . . . and didn't care.

Malik dialed Irvin's office.

"Hello," Irvin answered. "Give me two minutes. I'm

on my way out of the office now." Irvin gathered documents to show the president. The rumors of multiple assassination plots against him were real and in motion, according to the intelligence gathered. As he rounded the corner en route to the Oval Office, Irvin observed the president's economic advisor and other cabinet members speaking in hushed tones in a suspicious huddle outside the president's office. As he neared, the chatter quieted, then the group suddenly disbursed, headed in different directions.

"Good evening, gentlemen," Irvin cordially spoke in the midst of their departures.

They all casually waved. Irvin knocked, then entered the Oval Office, finding the president at his desk, staring out of the window in deep thought.

"What's on your mind, Malik?" he questioned.

"If I only knew where to start. There's really no beginning or end, just a political nightmare," Malik responded.

"How about I share with you what I've uncovered? Then we can make some decisions."

"That sounds like the best idea I've heard all morning."

"For starters, your economic team was in a suspicious huddle outside your door. What happened? You kicked them out?"

"Had to show them who was boss!"

"Did they believe you?"

"Fuck them. They believe in Wall Street and poll numbers."

"Sounds about right," Irvin said.

"What did you hear?"

"Those old, wrinkled, rich guys with mountains of wealth are launching a very expensive campaign against you and James."

"What's new?" Malik shot back.

"There are rampant discussions on the best way to eliminate you."

"That leaves me with two more years in office to make their lives a living hell, and their pockets will foot the bill," Malik joked.

"From what I'm gathering, they don't plan on waiting for those two years to end."

"That's too damn bad, 'cause I'm planning on being here," Malik answered.

"They seem to think you had something to do with the death of their friend George McNamara."

"Is that right? Just like many people think Lee Harvey Oswald wasn't behind the killing of John F. Kennedy. And they may be correct . . . if only they can prove it," Malik said.

"Many of George's constituents have seats in the Congress and Senate, and they want blood."

"Are they vampires?"

"No, just rich and powerful."

"So, you're insinuating that Washington's elite want me whacked?"

"Exactly! They feel it was their money that resulted in you being elected, and you have not lived up to their expectations."

"How serious are they?" Malik inquired.

"Very serious. The market has been losing billions

every day, and James has no plans on letting them in on his goose that lays golden eggs."

"Why should he?"

"I agree," Irvin said.

"What's our next move?"

"Protect the king. It's still chess."

"Where is he now?" Malik asked.

"On his way to the Fortress."

"What's my next move?"

"Continue moving about as if nothing is wrong. We're narrowing it down to their key players," Irvin assured him.

"How many from my cabinet?"

"A few, probably. Could be more. So for now, no trips outside of what you and I plan."

"Anything else I need to know?"

"James said to tell you he's very proud of you."

Malik smiled at the thought of an extraordinary man such as James being proud of him. If only he knew, it's because of him that he continued to embrace the presidency. Malik then thought of his wife who put her life on hold so that he could chase history, and the ambitions of a virtuous plan, consummated between friends. Would their marriage survive the constant dangers? Or would they both ultimately lose their lives in the process of holding on to ambitions? His smile left as fast as it appeared.

James sat in the helicopter in deep thought as it glided over the horizon that gave way to the magnificent view of the newly built fortress that took six months to build. The wall surrounding the Fortress was unusually tall and intimidating. The grounds were meticulously groomed and lined with exotic trees sprinkled about within the massive landscape expanding a mile in every direction.

Salvator, Joy, and General McCloud looked down in awe, as they now descended upon the launch pad built outside the large tunnel leading into the huge castlelike mansion.

The Fortress was an amazing sight to the others, yet James was convinced he'd seen this place before. He was sure of it, but he couldn't remember who owned it. There was an uncertain feeling that he'd been here before.

The Tomahawk landed; then everyone entered the tunnel by way of a minisubway car that escorted them the rest of their journey into the mansion. The scenery was stunning. The walls of the tunnels were murals, painted in correlation to the jungles of Africa. The colors were vivid and illuminated under soft, golden lighting that made the scenery come alive, as if you were on an African safari.

The scene seemed to bring back James's memory of the Fortress, and when he'd last seen it. He sat silently, deep in thought, then a tear rolled down his cheek. Then another. Then more followed.

Salvator sat across from his friend, observing, yet not knowing what he should do. The railcar came to an abrupt halt; then everyone stood up to leave. Joy jolted out of her daydream, then glanced at James, and did a double take when she noticed James's emotional state.

"What's wrong?" she gently asked.

James shook his head as if to say nothing. The truth was that he had trouble explaining it to himself. When he was in a coma, he remembered finding comfort in a place far, far away. The strength to endure, to fight another day existed in this place. For sure he recalled this fortress being that special place. He wept because he knew things he could not explain. He remembered being places but not knowing of how he'd gotten there. He remembered this fortress, but he couldn't remember how he entered it. It's as if everything was a sign that led to another piece of a puzzle he needed to put together, but not knowing why. This had James shaken because he had always been in control of his destiny. What did all this mean? Imhotep was a name he knew nothing of; yet, he knew it meant something. What did the name Gitalvo Gavinchi mean? What significance was the pink flower? Who were the familiar voices in hushed conversations? The giant that fell, he could not make out his face; yet it made him sad. What did these things represent, this big puzzle? James considered, as confused as ever.

"SURPRISE!" everyone yelled as James, Salvator, Joy, and General McCloud stepped through the doors. *What's the surprise?* James thought.

"How does it feel to be in your new home?" Luqman asked.

James was even more confused. "What do you mean my new home?"

"This is your brand-new fortress. State of the art. The

only one of its kind in the world, equipped with all the bells and whistles!" Luqman proudly stated.

"What you're saying is that I've never been here before?" James inquired, looking to his left, then to his right.

"Yep," Luqman replied.

"Impossible!" James insisted.

"What's that, James?" Deon questioned.

"I've been here before. I just don't know why or who owns this place. But I know who designed it," James said.

Luqman looked at James as if he'd lost his mind. "There's only one man who could design this place, and nobody knew of this special design but him. You sure you're feeling okay?" Luqman questioned.

"One hundred percent sure. How about you?" James asked in a slightly irritated manner.

"Okay, James. I'm going to write down the name of the designer of this fortress, then give it to Deon. Then we'll see if you're correct."

Luqman scribbled on a piece of paper, then handed it to Deon. "Ready when you are, James," he confidently said.

"He's from England, and his name is Gitalvo Gavinchi," James said.

Luqman's jaw dropped open after hearing the answer. "How did you know that?"

"Don't know, I just do. I told you I'd been here before. I can tell you about every room here, along with its contents, from the artwork to the ancient artifacts. In the library, there's a book lying on the desk. Can you retrieve it for me, Luqman?"

"Yeah, right." Luqman snickered. "Can you tell me where the library is?"

"Three doors to your right, take a left, then another right," James stated.

Once Luqman had left, James scribbled on a sheet of paper the name of the book and where the bookmark marked the page. Everyone stood in wonder of what was going on, because explaining it was too far-fetched.

Luqman strolled back into the room, carrying a book. Deon reached for the book to check the information James had given her moments earlier. Her facial expression told the entire story. James had once again amazed them as she passed the slip of paper around the room, along with the book. Everyone now turned to James, wondering what was going on.

"The bookmarker should be on page twenty-nine," James stated. "Within the third paragraph it reads: '*In order to find a treasure, you will have to follow the omens. God has prepared a path for everyone to follow. You just have to read the omens that he left for you.*'"

Luqman looked through the book, finding exactly where James said it was marked, then read the paragraph to himself. He looked up from the book, then nodded, indicating James was right again.

"How do you know these things, James?"

"I told you. I don't know, but things are becoming clear now that I'm here," he expressed.

"What things are becoming clear?" Salvator questioned.

"To realize one's purpose is a person's only obligation,

and when you want something, the universe conspires in helping you to achieve it," he said.

"So, what exactly are you saying you feel you need to achieve?" Deon asked.

"That's why I'm leaving for Africa tomorrow in search of something," James confessed.

Everyone held looks of confusion and concern. Nobody understood any of the latest twists from James, but this was catastrophic to their plans.

"What's in Africa?" Luqman questioned.

"That's what I'm going to find out."

"But what about what's going on with this company, James? These are some critical times! We need you!" Deon pleaded.

"Salvator will take over where I'm needed. We've had the last few months to go over strategies."

"Is Africa that important?" Joy inquired.

"Not unless you can explain what you just saw and heard?"

Truth is, nobody knew what was going on. They were just as lost as James, without any explanation why. James felt the tension in the air, thick enough to cut. But in his heart, he knew leaving for Africa in search of the pieces to the big puzzle in his mind was the key. He now understood that he received an omen. The answer to this trivia could prevent something, or invent his next big move. All his life, he relied on instinct. Yet, this time, the force was more powerful, more deliberate, and more divine. It simply couldn't be ignored. This time, it felt as if his destiny was attached to his decision.

"Look, as eerie as all this is sounding, it's real. I know much is going on with the business, and you guys are doing an excellent job. But you're going to have to trust me on this one. For some strange reason, I feel this is my destiny. I also think the direction of our legacy depends on whatever becomes of this trip," James insisted.

"What do you want to be done about the Saul Deblanco situation?" Salvator asked.

"Let's get with Hector Satorie and move on Saul as soon as you learn of his whereabouts. I want his fuckin' head in a jar—immediately!" James demanded.

"What about Don Santos and the Commission?"

"Let's first see exactly what their little meeting was about. If there was no definite order to move on us, then let's play it by ear. But in case we need to take them out at a moment's notice, put a tail on their movements. Don Santos also. He has separated himself from the others, but the Trojan horse worked in Troy, and it's a point well taken. What's going on with Julio?"

"He received a visit from Agent John Cage the other day," Tray informed him.

"So, what's our next move?"

"We have a cobra on the inside, ready to strike," Tray admitted.

"Very good. The sooner, the better," James replied. "How's business, Deon?"

"Busy, busy," she said with a sigh.

"Is that good or bad?"

"Both!"

"Why is that?"

"Need more plants built to keep up with the demand for our vehicles."

"We're out of money?" James asked with sarcasm.

"Not money, just personnel!" Deon aggressively stated. "Look, James, everybody has been pulling a hell of a load since you left, and the loads continue to get heavier as time goes by. We're basically working 24/7 nonstop. On top of that, our lives are in danger. So hiring people is tedious . . . not to mention a dangerous process when anyone could be a potential threat."

"Then call Irvin and have him screen some trustworthy people with CEO credentials that he's personally acquainted with."

"See, that's why you're needed here. You know what to do in every aspect about the business," Troy added.

"That's what you're used to, Troy. In order to be a leader, you have to lead. You must trust your decision-making ability, and then it'll become second nature. Remember this, and it's important for everyone to understand my point. On every team, the leader has to trust the other players on the team. Michael Jordan didn't win a single championship by himself, and I can't run this company by myself. There's no doubt that we're a championship-caliber team, and the world knows it. There isn't a person on the globe who has never heard of Johnson Industries. That's us! And we better damn sure know we belong where we are. We can get a yes from anyone we deal with right now, knowing the answer should've been no. Now *that's* power! From this position we don't ask; we *demand*, or we *destroy*! *That's* who we are," James stated.

Everyone sat silent and marveled at how James conducted himself as he had so many times in the past. At that moment, they knew nothing was wrong with James mentally. He was just as sharp — if not sharper — than before the coma. They had to believe in James's omens. It would be foolish not to. Yet, they had missed him dearly. They thought he was home to stay. Things just weren't the same without the brutally honest wisdom of their leader. He had been the constant in their lives. He was their friend, their brother, their father, and whatever else they needed him to be for the moment. He held the title faithfully. It grieved them to lose him again.

Yet amongst them, another threat was lurking. As everyone was gathered around to regroup, Joy's phone was vibrating continuously. She casually seated herself in a corner chair, then retrieved the phone. The word: URGENT appeared across the screen.

On the other side of the room, Salvator curiously monitored Joy's fidgety behavior. He strolled across the room to check on her. At the sight of Salvator, she instantly slipped the phone back in her pocket, then stood up.

"How's it going?" he asked.

"Never better," she lied, returning his piercing gaze.

"That bad, huh?"

"Yep. How about you?" she asked, waving at James, who managed to look over at them while talking to Luqman and Deon.

"I have no life other than the obvious," he said.

"And exactly what is 'the obvious'?"

He stared for a moment, having an intuitive conviction that something was unsound. "Protect the king," he said in a hushed tone.

"Of course," Joy said, shifting her weight from one leg to another, even being well aware of Salvator's ability to read body language.

As Salvator was turning to walk away, Joy's phone began to vibrate once more. He stopped in his tracks. They both stood in silence.

"Are you going to answer that?" he curiously asked while slightly turning his body toward her.

"Naah, it's nothing," she struggled to get out, trying to keep her composure as her legs went dead. "The chancellor at the university wants to know when I'll be returning."

Salvator looked over at Joy with raised eyebrows and a crooked grin. He knew she had lied to him at least twice today. He straightened his all-black signature suit and adjusted his black tie . . . as the phone began to vibrate once more.

"That's a very persistent chancellor, Ms. Turner," he stated as he turned and walked away.

Chapter 22

Diamond was driving the new Audi A8 down Canal Street looking for her cousin Carla at the Popeyes chicken on the corner of Galvez and Canal streets. She blew the horn, gaining Carla's attention as she stood outside the popular restaurant with what looked like enough chicken to feed an army. Immediately, Carla began waving her hand in the air like a tourist flagging down a taxi. Diamond pulled to the curb; then Carla jumped in and immediately gave her cousin a big hug.

"Damn, girl, let my neck go," Diamond insisted.

"You know I missed you, Diamond. Why you trippin'?"

"Because of the bear hug you laid on me with them big-ass arms, girl. Look at you. What the hell, you trying to become a bouncer?"

"Yo' ass just getting small. Nothing wrong with this healthy diva. You trippin'!" Carla expressed, smacking her lips with her hands on her wide hips.

"Baby, remind me to buy you another scale, 'cause the one you have is off by a landslide. However, how's my aunt, and how much did you tell her?"

"I keep it a hundred with moms, Dee. I'd told her I'm with you, and, no, I didn't say where we were headed, but she knows I'm in good hands, and so are you. She sends her love, nonetheless."

"Where are you going with that hundred-piece box of chicken, girl?"

"I'm going to eat it, if that's okay with you. Girl, this that extra spicy too. And just came out of the grease, piping hot. So stop acting like you wasn't raised on this," Carla said.

"I must admit it's good to be back home and all, but not enough to go on an eating binge, then mess up this perfect figure."

"Girl, pulleeese. Yo' skinny ass don't have no damn figure. Stop dreaming and let me in on this plan of yours."

"Well, as you know, I've opened my stores in Atlanta, but we're going to take this to another level. We have two things in our way: Kane and the people chasing him."

"You sho' is right, girl," Carla responded.

"Kane isn't going to change his lifestyle; it's what makes him tick. He'll die by the same code willingly, and if the dope game ceased to exist, he'd die of a broken heart. He loves the game more than me, and I can't allow his fate to become mine. This is why I'm going to capitalize on the opportunity being presented," Diamond said, now holding her hand up for a high five.

"You know I'm with you, win, lose, or draw."

"I know, Carla. And trust me, it's going to be greater later."

"You make it sound like we're into some serious shit, girl!"

"Very serious, Carla. Peep this. Don't think this move is about the broad Tara. She and her baby have my blessings, victims of circumstances. This move is more about

Kane's betrayal of my love and trust. I went against my better judgment in support of him by placing my life in danger as I knew major people were hot on his trail, threatening to body him, and, no doubt, me too if I was there when they came. I know Kane's a street nigga, and hoes are a part of the equation. Yet, the sin wasn't that he had hoes; it's the fact of him being caught. I doubt he explored the possibility of me catching him, or what I'd do next. That'll prove to be his biggest mistake. He, of all people, should know, in the game of numbers, you must account for everything and everybody. He underestimated me; I won't make the same mistake," Diamond said.

Diamond pulled into the parking garage at Canal Place. She navigated the Audi around the circular ramp until she found a parking spot.

"Where we goin'?" Carla asked.

"We're gonna spend a little money. I'm going to be here for about a week in preparation for my next move."

Carla smiled with raised eyebrows. "What move is that?"

"The double cross," Diamond assured her, the words sounding more deliberate and sinister rolling off her tongue.

"Let me in on it, girl!" Carla excitedly said as they strolled into Saks Fifth Avenue to do some shopping.

"It's simple. I'm going to set up a meeting with Troy and Luqman. They're businessmen."

"Who's that?"

"Those were the dudes pulling up at the house in the Hummer. They were picking up the money from Kane."

"Okay, I see now. You don't think that'll be kinda dangerous?"

"If they find me before I find them, *that* will be dangerous. I'm going to reach out to them, set up a meeting, then possibly get rich off Kane's whereabouts. What you think?"

"I think it's brilliant. How much are you asking for?"

"Maybe I'll just let them make me an offer. Besides, I get all the dope and money left behind too."

"How much is that?" Carla asked, being nosy.

"Over one hundred kilos and a couple million."

"Damn, girl! They're not gonna want their stuff back?"

"How would they know if anything's left? Kane sells dope, remember?"

"Exactly!" Carla said.

"Look, pick out something nice and sexy. We're setting up a meeting for tonight. We'll go somewhere with plenty of lights and surveillance."

"Let's go to Harrah's Casino," Carla suggested.

"That's perfect! Be quiet. I'm giving Troy a call now," Diamond stated.

"Hello?" Troy answered.

"Troy, this is Diamond. We need to talk."

"It's been a long time, Diamond. I thought we were bigger than that," Troy said.

"That's why I'm calling you."

"So, what's really going on?"

"It's business, and you're a businessman the last I checked," Diamond confidently spoke.

"Who are you representing?"

"Myself," she expressed with emphasis.

"The last time I checked, you had a teammate."

"Naah, I was on a team; there's a big difference."

"So, there's no more team?"

"Not yet, but I'm working on it. Nothing wrong with me having my own, huh?"

"That depends," Troy shot back.

"On what?"

"On whether you're smart like you confessed."

"Only time will tell, huh?"

"Are you inquiring about how much time you have left?" Troy questioned.

"Maybe, or maybe I'm trying to buy some."

"That sounds like a very smart move on your part, being I was real close to finalizing my mission in the ATL, if you know what I mean," Troy threatened, making sure the information seeped into her mind that he knew exactly where they laid their heads.

The information scared Diamond. She knew she had to come back strong to save face.

"I was told that the greatest warriors were the ones who humbled themselves," she began. "I've paid attention to you more than even you could imagine, Troy. No, I'm not surprised nor amazed that your mission was close to being finalized," Diamond lied. "But more importantly, the respect I have for you has brought me to the table today. I also know that the man and woman can live on that which they stand on, provided their proven words speak for them," she said.

"And what would your words say to me?" Troy questioned.

"That I follow the rules."

"Whose rules?"

"The rules."

"Oh yeah?"

"Look, Troy. I was a good wife, and I did what a loyal wife does . . . stand by her man. I followed the rules, just like I said. I would have stood by my man's side till our caskets dropped, but as fate would have it, another ending is in order."

"So, let me guess. Only one casket deserves to drop now?"

"If that's the hand fate deals, who can prevent it?" Diamond inquired.

"What do you want from me?"

"Meet me in an hour at Harrah's Casino at the bar and bring a friend to keep mine company," Diamond pitched.

"You got that, Ms. Diamond. We'll see you then."

Troy hung up the phone. He and Luqman looked at each other, puzzled about the conversation they'd heard over the speakerphone.

"What do you think?" Troy asked.

"Can't really say. I think we'll find out in about an hour."

"How did you think she took the information about us knowing they're in Atlanta?"

"Probably a blessing."

"At any rate, we can't miss out on this opportunity, if that's what it is," Troy considered.

Diamond and Carla were getting dressed in their penthouse suite at the "W" across the street from Harrah's Casino. Both women were casually dressed in blue jeans and a Vivian Dolanski blouse, accentuated with Prada heels and purses. The two women were gorgeous, and would easily be the sexiest at the bar at this time of day. With about fifteen minutes until showtime, they powdered their noses as if auditioning for *America's Next Top Model*.

"It's showtime, girl! How do I look?" Diamond asked, posing in the giant mirror on the wall.

"Almost as good as me," Carla smiled.

"Be serious for once in your life, girl."

"Girl, you straight, with your skinny self."

"If you say so," Diamond said. "However, this meeting is a very critical component in my overall plan. I must come across as trustworthy. My future depends on it."

"So, what do you need me to do?" Carla questioned with a bit of reluctance.

"Watch my back—always," Diamond shot back, emphasizing the serious nature of her words.

"What do you mean?"

"Pay attention. No matter how insignificant it may seem, never forget it, nor not react to it. I need to know everything you know, or think, and definitely witness. Trust me; it'll keep us safe," Diamond demanded.

"You got that, cuz."

"Are you sure?"

"Trust me. I got you."

"Look, don't get caught up in your conversation with his friend, Luqman, and don't forget your behavior from a business standpoint. You see, a genuine perception by him will play a big role in Troy's final decision. This is my reason for bringing you along. Troy respects Luqman's input unconditionally," Diamond assured her.

"I think I can be genuine."

"Well, let's get out of here then."

The women rode the elevator down to the first floor, strolled out of the hotel, then across the street into Harrah's Casino. They were now seated at the bar, enjoying a laugh . . . when their attention suddenly was diverted toward two tall, handsome gentlemen standing in front of them draped in expensive, tailored, Armani suits. There was also a huge bodyguard standing to their far left, attempting to be inconspicuous.

Diamond's mind raced at full speed as she stood taken aback by the power that emanated from the two men. She had never seen them dressed this way, nor with bodyguards. This most definitely added another dimension to her plan.

Troy locked eyes with Diamond for what seemed like an eternity, cautiously peeping into the windows of her soul, searching for anything abnormal that would quickly cost her, her life. Then he extended his hand. She accepted, wearing a smile that was both genuine and irresistible to the average man.

"Ladies, why don't you both join us?" Troy offered, ushering them to a table.

"I think you met my partner, right?"

"Nice to see you again, Luqman," Diamond warmly expressed.

"The pleasure is all mine," he replied.

"Troy, Luqman, this is my partner, Carla," Diamond said.

"As in business partner?"

"Exactly," Diamond answered.

"So, what exactly is your business?"

"Beauty products."

"This is news to me," Troy said.

"I've always wanted to own a successful business, but circumstances wedged its way in between that one . . . for a time."

"You speak as if you've eliminated those circumstances."

"In a way I have. Yet, in a way, I haven't. That's why I'm here today."

"How may I assist you then?" Troy questioned.

"I have access to someone you want, and you have something I need."

Troy studied Diamond for thirty seconds. "Would you two excuse us for a moment?" Troy suggested, then rose from his chair. He walked around to Diamond's chair, then slid it back like the perfect gentleman. "Take a walk with me," he leaned in and whispered into Diamond's ear.

From out of nowhere, another bodyguard appeared. He had been seated in the back of the bar. Upon Troy's signal, the bodyguard was now leading the way. Once outside, the door to their stretch limo Hummer was opened, with the chauffer standing beside it.

Diamond glanced at Troy curiously when they approached the Hummer. Troy nodded. She reluctantly stepped in, then the door was closed behind them. The chauffeur and the bodyguard stood outside. Troy looked deeply into Diamond's eyes, then aggressively gave her a command.

"Take off your clothes!"

"For what?" Diamond questioned, a bit agitated by the request.

"Look at it as an initiation," Troy shot back, not cracking a smile.

Diamond began calculating the risks versus the rewards of not complying. *But what's his angle? Is this just for some free pussy? Probably not.* Whatever it is, she had to pass the tests. Her life depended on it.

Slowly, she began to peel off the layers of expensive clothing. Troy sat back in the Hummer tuned in to every move. Truth being, he had to know if she was wearing a wire.

Diamond now sat in her Victoria's Secret bra and panties, with her eyes trained on Troy like a cobra ready to strike. Troy continued to observe without speaking another word. She suddenly turned her back toward him, then held up her long dreads so that he could unbuckle her bra. A few seconds passed without Troy saying a word, so Diamond abruptly turned around.

"You can put your clothes back on. I'm not a rapist."

"Never figured you to be that in my wildest imagination," Diamond stated.

"So just what have you figured out that led you to me?"

"It's as simple as I stated earlier. You scratch my back, and I scratch yours. I have someone you want; you have something I need."

"So, that's the million-dollar question?" Troy inquired.

"Isn't it obvious?" she asked.

"Not really," Troy quipped.

"How much is it worth to you?"

"Depends on what you're figuring to get."

"Maybe it's best you come up with a reasonable offer."

"Look, Diamond, Kane's worth to me is next to nothing. Surely, I can walk away from this situation and lose no business or sleep. What he took helped him, and it didn't hurt me. It was that insignificant. However, if what you're attempting to come out of this with is legitimate, then what you can accomplish will be worth much more than what Kane's worth to me," Troy assured her.

"So, exactly what would you be offering, Troy?"

"My good graces," he shot back.

Diamond leaned back in the comfortable seat, catching the threat Troy just threw. Although he didn't say it, it was accurately communicated through the unreadable face Diamond was looking into. Now painted into a corner, she had to respect the power before her . . . or buck it.

Troy counted to ten in his mind, then reached for the door handle.

"What do you want to know?" Diamond questioned, knowing the possibility of her leaving the vehicle—or Troy's clutches—weren't good.

He eased his hand off the handle, then leaned back in the seat, now satisfied that Diamond chose to live.

"I need to know everything," Troy said.

To be continued . . .